Story of a Story
and Other Stories:
A Novel

By Stephen Dixon

Novels:

Work (1977)
Too Late (1978)
Fall & Rise (1985)
Garbage (1988)
Frog (1991)
Interstate (1995)
Gould (1997)
30: Pieces of a Novel (1999)
Tisch (2000; written 1961-1969)
I. (2002)
Old Friends (2004)
Phone Rings (2005)
End of I. (2006)
Meyer (2007)

Story collections:

No Relief (1976)
Quite Contrary: The Mary and Newt Story (1979)
14 Stories (1980)
Movies: Seventeen Stories (1983)
Time to Go (1984)
The Play and Other Stories (1988)
Love and Will: Twenty Stories (1989)
All Gone: 18 Short Stories (1990)
Friends: More Will and Magna Stories (1990)
Long Made Short (1994)
The Stories of Stephen Dixon (1994)
Man on Stage: Play Stories (1996)
Sleep (1999)
*What Is All This?: The Uncollected Stories
of Stephen Dixon* (2010)

4.10.12

SOASAOS: AN was a novel I wrote 40 years ago, tried to get it published for a couple of years, got some unflattering rejections for a change — before they were always gracious and "not right for us" and "wouldn't know how to market this" and "hope you have better luck with it with another publisher..." If accepted, it would have been my FIRST published book. At the time I had about 8 published stories, in both little & big magazines.

I put it away for about 20 years, discovered it where I'd left it — in a satchel of unpublished novels — rewrote (more like fixed up) just a little of it, & decided to send it out again. A small publisher took it, even copyedited it, & then denied it had taken it. I only sent it to one.

I put it away for another 20 years, thought I'd lost it, discovered where I'd left it — in a briefcase of forgotten unpublished stories — & decided to send it out again. Fortunately (The only place I sent it to was Fugue State Press. The illustration on the cover is as old as the novel. The photo of my typewriter is new.

Story of a Story and Other Stories: A Novel

by

Stephen Dixon

fugue state press
new york

Library of Congress Control Number 2012933135

ISBN 978-1-879193-27-7

Front cover painting by Stephen Dixon;
back cover photo by Sophia Dixon

Published by Fugue State Press
PO Box 80, Cooper Station
New York NY 10276

www.fuguestatepress.com
info@fuguestatepress.com

Story of a Story
and Other Stories:
A Novel

SOASAOS: AN

"Shelly called," his mother says. "She was very concerned about Dad and what Sis is doing in Italy. She left her Rhode Island phone number and French address and said if you don't call immediately then write her in Paris, as her living schedule's been switched and she instead now spends her winters overseas."

"So long, Paul," Shelly says. "How's your work coming? Better yet, what are your plans for the Labor Day weekend? Alain and I would love seeing you, and Sharon will go wild for her scribbling man. Gather a few clothes quick, don't forget a swimsuit, leave right away and you can be here by nine. I'll prepare a luscious supper, though I've nothing in the fridge. Alain won't be here till tomorrow, which means you can ride back with us if you don't want to drive your heap. Monday's holiday and Tuesday's when I have to be at my New York back doctor and Wednesday you can see me off on the *France*. In fact, maybe you will have to drive your minibus up, as I'm taking an orthopedic double bed to Paris and it might not fit on Alain's rack. But I'll be waiting for you no matter what hour you arrive. And I promise to be on my best behavior this time and to you especially nice."

"Nah," his mother says. "You deserve to get away. I deserve to get away also, but I'll see to Dad all right. It's unhealthy your hanging around older people so much. I'll make you a sandwich for the trip. Make it yourself then, but be sure it's on my homemade rye. I'd sharpen that knife first, as the bread's so fresh it'll dissolve the blade. Drive carefully, dear, hear?"

"Sure, you know you're doing?" his father says. "We were hoping you'd drive us to my niece's one day this weekend, though it's okay. Stay safe. No strangers. Who's Shelly?"

The sign on the highway on-ramp says NO. The Vermont car in front of him has for a license plate number TORAH. The electric sign in the back window of the car he's behind signals NO TAILGAITING...TRAFFIC JAM AHEAD... WHERE'S THE FIRE?...PASS ON MY LEFT PLEASE...HAVE A TOPNOTCH DAY... and then YOU'RE WELCOME to the THANK YOU of the automatic tollbooth.

The hitchhiker Paul picks up says he's been given a substantial advance for a travel book he's writing on how to bum across America and back with only a five-spot in your pocket and return to college in the fall with the same five-dollar bill and change. "Trick's to thumb all the way while worming into your drivers' houses to eat, thief and sleep with their daughters and wives. Sneak into campsites at night if you can't your last driver's home. Sad-tale the drivers into buying your food on the road and your camp neighbors your provisions in the parks. Get your clean clothes from unattended Laundromat dryers, your reading matter by snitching it off the stands, and your petty cash by fingering behind the cushions of the cars you're in. But to juice up the book I've snapped a thousand sunshady shots of my different-featured drivers and their cargos and cars, created anecdotes as to how this one tried to bugger and mug me and some other viper duped me into downing the most mind-mowing dope, and recounted the truth about my eventually letting this itzy missy seduce me in the back of her Bentley and then with her three bookish girlfriends for a week lavishly fete and teat me at her private lakeside palazzo. But seeing you're in too much of a rush to stop and treat me to my feedbag tonight, can you put me up for free wherever you're heading or drop me off with a spare ducatoon or two at the next service stop?"

Shelly's leaning out of her second-story window as he pulls up. "I heard your bus blustering some ten blocks from here. How goes it? Why so few new lines on your graven face? Does our silly village still seem to you the same pretty picture postcard sane?"

They eat and drink, make for the master bedroom where she has a new bigger-than-kingsize bed. "Handcarved by our local carpentry craftsmen," she says, "though not the bed voyaging to France. Tell me more of your fruitful junior high school teaching experiences this year."

"I got a meaty short story out of it and enough berries and lettuce, etcetera, stashed away to write without working for three months."

Sharon cries from the next room. Shelly motions him to be silent, comforts her child.

"Daddy didn't come?"

"Tomorrow, sweet."

"I thought I heard voices."

"They were probably some of your dream characters, originating from that nightmarish bedtime story you insisted I read. You can fall asleep without me, can't you? Then sleep."

Paul had put his pants on and was back on the couch reading.

"Creative thinking," Shelly says. "Shall we try again?"

"Well, I feel eight times as foolish by making the long trek from antechamber couch to quadruple fourposter twice in two minutes."

"Why not sixteen times? Thirty-two?" Later: "*Doucement*, Paul, *doucement*." Later: "It's always amusing what stories couples will tell each other after sex." Later: "Well I feel fulfilled sexually, shouldn't I be two?" Later: "I've typed these directions to get to my studio, as I usually confound more than I instruct when I verbally explain."

3 blocks N along Salters Grove, then W at Brook to #2. Pull string on rt side of doubledoored gate & push left side while latch is raised. 1st door along path on rt side is studio entrance, 2nd door's your downstairs neighbors & my wellpaying lessee. She's a widowed invalid with a moribund heart, ulcerated legs, understandably caustic disposition & live-in deafmute maid, doty schnauzer & numerous photos of her never-visiting colorless children & grandchild on top of a remote control color TV. I've already incorporated her situation in an accepted short story, so suggest not writing about it without changing the dog's breed & infirmities of tenant & nurse. Turn on hallway switch at left to get upstairs.

"It doesn't say how I turn the hallway switch off."

"You can't unless you come downstairs again. And then you won't be able to reclimb the still-obstructed stairs without breaking your neck or turning the downstairs light back on."

Walk 1 flt up—softly, preferably shoelessly, as Mrs. G's quite ill & Lassie sleeps light. You'll see a small fridge on 2nd landing. Don't put perishable items inside as it's unplugged & full of mold & there's no outlet nearby. Alain tried carrying it to the studio, but couldn't get it beyond the 2nd fl. Maybe you could help him with it while you're here.

"Tomorrow morning I'll get the refrigerator up by myself."

It's very heavy & still quite new, so don't try lifting up upstairs yourself. Continue along rt to 3rd landing. Raise left arm while standing on top step & you'll find studio lightswitch string. Raise rt arm & you'll have both arms raised. Linens in bureau, pillows on settee. Can you make your own bed? Goodnight. Sleeptight.

Last time he was in this village was two winters ago when for a month he lived alone on the first floor in what's now her tenant's flat. About a week into his stay Shelly started storming into his rooms complaining he was scratching the floors, the building's consuming too much oil for one man, why must he move furniture around all hours of the night? And the cooking smells. "Alain's been mentioning these obnoxious kitchen odors and I now know what he means. Don't you ever open the windows? What do you think the ventilating fan's for? Must you cook everything with garlic and scallions and brew all your drinks with cinnamon and cloves? And you must try making friends with the mop and broom we've provided. Dust collects on the baseboards and wainscots and can leave hairy clusters in the corners and homely gray stains on the floor. And next time you can't get your jalop started, don't ask my handyman upstairs to help. I pay him more in a quarter-hour than it would cost me to call the most luxurious garage around here to give you a push. And look at the marks you've made on the new cabinets, walls and doors. We were counting on renting this place for the summer and hopefully year-round. Now it'll need a new coat when it's been freshly painted and the floors will have to be resanded, finished and waxed." He left without telling them, leaving behind the housekeys, fifty-dollar check for utility expenses, that they never cashed, and a note apologizing for the hardships he might have caused them and a PS questioning her project to set up a writers colony in this village and the justness of their complaints. First time he heard from either of them since then was her phone call today.

Shelly calls. "Morning. Sleep tight? Dreams right? Come for breakfast."

"Paulie," Sharon says, wheeing through the house to him, kissing his lips while her legs strangle his waist. "And how's my friend the Multimal?"

"Sent his best wishes from the hospital, where he was laid up for a few months."

"That's right. I got your postcards. What's he there for again?"

"Lost one of his tails and he needs five to fly. And despite the cheerful room and nurses, he got tired of the doctors postponing his operation till a rare six-tailed multimal might happen to check in for a tail removal, so he decided to escape from the hospital instead."

"Why didn't he fly away with his four tails?"

"Because he already has four mouths and you know a multimal can't have the same number of any two parts of his body. That's why he only has one ear, two noses, three nostrils, four mouths, five tails, six legs, seven horns, eight eyes, nine hooves and ten tongues. So yesterday he slipped out by dressing up like a doctor in a surgeon's mask and racing to the roof and sliding down the eleven flights of drainpipe and wobbling away."

"Seems absurd when he could've asked to be discharged or took the elevator to the lobby and left. Where'd he go, though?"

"Hailed a cab to my folks' place, where he's at now."

"Your mom doesn't mind?"

"He helps out, bakes great cakes, wheels my pop to the park when I'm not home and will escort my mother to the latest operas and ettas I don't like."

"How is your father?"

Alain arrives from New York. They sit down for lunch. "Tell Paul about Vivian's suicide last month," he says.

"It was like being mashed against rocks. I slept the entire day of the funeral so I wouldn't have to go. She did it so insanely. Not because of that. She attempted three times before—gas, pills and a plastic dry-cleaning bag. She was my best friend. Her husband Oliver kept on salvaging her. Why'd you bring it up? She was so gifted. She opened Hemingway's collected short stories to the story "Fathers and Sons" alluding to his own father shooting himself. Now that I think of it, there was that Turgenev novel, which they were both familiar with, of course. Something about their use of a known title eludes me, hers more than Hem's, as she had a daughter, and in that story he did promise us and ultimately deliver more on his father's suicide later on. But with her two-year-old in the crib to watch the final scene not a foot from the writing table Vivian sat behind—"

"We're not sure Ruby was up when Vi died."

"The report surely got her up. But you'll see why I think she was, Paul. With the collection opened to his suicide allusion and on the same table, her own that-day completed manuscript turned to the page where the lady writer in the story blows half her head off with a double-barreled Boss shotgun, she slipped six shells into her father's old 32-cal revolver, lowered the gun butt on the table, sat forward, placed the barrel dead center against her forehead just above the eyebrows and tripped the trigger. When Oliver came home he also thought Ruby had been killed, since she had so much of her mother's blood on her face and was sleeping so soundly. The blood's reason one why I think Ruby saw. She was probably standing in her crib and resting her head on the rail as she did—whole head on top, chin on the back of her hands interlocked, scrutinizing events and objects for hours and which I once borrowed her in a story for. Now she never says a word but boom-boom and dada and won't look at anything from that crib position but the ceiling and floor. Before, the only words she spoke regularly were momma and bow-wow."

Shelly gives Paul a manuscript of a novel she recently finished. It's 110 pages. Some pages only have one line, two just one word, no page has more than six lines. "In all," she says, "it can be read by the average reader in half an hour, with most of the book's action being in turning the pages. If a reader has poor manipulative control, the reading will take longer. If he really wants it to be a long drawn-out novel, he can turn the pages with his nose. In many respects the reader writes most of the novel himself, both in his head and on interspersed blank pages. On the blank title page he's supplied with a small sharpened pencil with my name on it and 'compliments of the publisher,' though I'm sure the difference of the book selling for seven dollars rather than six ninety-five, and where he's invited to write his own name and either guess at or return later to give the book its title. The dust jacket will also be bare, except for an exact-size photo of the pencil in front turned to the lettering and one of those Band-Aid-like pieces of tape on back where the reader can tear off the protective paper from the adhesive and stick on a snapshot of himself. The jacket's front fold-in will be where he can synopsize the book and write promotional blurbs, and the back fold where he can list some of his past accomplishments, professions, book titles, residences, marital status and names of his spouse, children and pets. On the succeeding blank pages past the flyleaf, spaced about fifteen pages apart, the reader's asked to draw or write a sketch of what he thinks the main characters look like or even say what he thinks of that suggestion, write in dialogue he feels I left out for overeager reasons of concision, and predict what the fates of the two main characters will be, and on the next-to-last blank page, should have been, if he does think there were two main characters. Naturally he's requested at the beginning of the book to edit or excise whatever he thinks is clumsy, boring, pretentious, verbose, unnecessarily digressive, redundant and worse. The last blank page is where the reader's given one more shot at defacing the book and lowering its resale value further, if he actually isn't the illustrious literary name he might have inscribed on the title page, by writing a one-word expletive as an opinion of the book. My final suggestion will be that the book owner pass the book on to someone else for corrections and opinions of his writing, editing and criticism. For library copies of the book I'd like double the number of blank pages at the same intervals and that the pencils be longer and have erasers and there be many more stickers for authors' pictures. Since I figure the end result will be my having written only half this novel, I can only accept that share of its censure, payments and praise. So half of whatever money I get for the book will be split between our village library and an urban hospital program specializing in the treatment and research of manic-depression and both in Vi's name."

"I wanted her to give that latter share to Ruby," Alain says. "But Shelly feels that getting book royalties and advances before one's even written a novel will only encourage Ruby to become a writer, a career we both feel because of nature she should for her life's sake doggedly avoid."

Paul reads her novel in 30 minutes. He writes "French name for 'title page'" on the title page and signs it "Nom de Plume." On an opinion page he writes "Too much French spoken if English isn't their natural tongue. What does dit-donc mean and moulinette? Advise substituting 'appointment' for the 'rendezvous' the dentist makes for his future patient. Why's the woman's 9-year-old daughter named 'Sharon' and her husband 'Alain,' unless you're planning to dedicate the novel to your husband and daughter, 'Artur and Marta.' Is Baron Soso a man or dog and not just because Shelly keeps flinging him bisquits and makes him drink his beverages from a bowl on the floor marked Chien. The sun sets in the West, even when one stands on his head in the rain in the southern hemisphere. You wrote that 'Shelly's greatest efforts were expended for the sake of man's soulful aspirations,' while to me her dominant drives seem to be to derange the daughter, dismay her husband, denude her lover, defrock her minister, devour her dinners, demoralize or domesticate Baron Soso and become the first female French premier so she can use its nuclear arsenal to demolish Western Europe, and the premier's 4-billion-Franc fallout shelter to become the last lady left in France."

He begins writing a story. "Sylvia called. Peter was surprised to hear from her after three years. 'How'd you like spending Labor Day weekend with Arthur, Marta, Siddhartha and Father and I on Author's Isle?'"

Shelly yells up the stairway, "Paul, may I come up?"

"A *moulinette* can only be a *moulinette*," she says, "while *dit-donc* might be translated as 'say there' or 'by the way,' though Alain Novel would never say either of those. How would it sound for a Frenchman to say 'Say there, your friend is a bit of a fiend, wouldn't you say?' Baron Soso's an ocelot and while I was in Paris I couldn't find a feed bowl in any pet store with the word *ocelot* on it. The sun sets in the East because that scene takes place in a dream. I like the name Sharon, which is why I chose it for my real daughter. The dedications are in rather than of the book by my naming its two most endearing characters after my daughter and husband. Some of it's wrong as you point out, but fortunately the manuscript can be rewritten in two hours and I've an excellent typist." She gives him a short story of hers she wants him to read immediately.

He reads, she bathes. It's about a sculptor's wife whose suddenly-famous husband is leaving her for a much younger woman after 20 years. She meets a writer at an art patron's party for her husband, which she isn't invited to, but summoned from home to patch up one of her husband's lifesized corduroy doors before the TV news team sets up. The writer's obviously Paul. He and Shelly met in Central Park in the filmmaker's contingent of a Stop the War march. In his pocket is the same-named male magazine with his story inside that on that March day had also come out on the stands. Percival's first words to her in her story are "A lot of men must want to fuck you because you're the wife of Juan." "Nobody wants to fuck me." "I do." "Then be my guest," and she leads him to one of Juan's giant softcovers in the patron's sculpture garden, opens it with her passkey and they crawl inside. The book's "*Austin's Pride and Prejudice.*" She describes their lovemaking like this: "The first time was a trifle theatrical, like a blustery old minor poet shouting and thrashing his poems during a stage reading to compensate for their tedium and stodginess. The second time was more relaxed, soft and eloquent, as if a poet laureate was reciting his most lyrical works before his respectful peers. Sheltered and warm, it stumps me why I didn't come."

"Your characters curse too much," Paul says, "and Percival's too much the schmo."

"That's right, I did sort of model him after you. But nothing personal that isn't generally known or publicly owned. And you can't be the only man with a VW bus, literary lust, makes vainglorious first passes and lived in the Rhode Island hills between two state troopers' homes which were lit up at night like concentration camps and patrolled by snapping K-9 dogs."

"A writer I know who's writing a story about a writer has been using some of the experiences I've told him of myself. The last one he apologized for having included in his piece concerns my having submitted a story to a literary review that's put out by a trade publishing house and getting back instead of my story and rejection slip a large check, minus the ten percent fee sent to my agent, and the galleys to a book called *The Gay American Cookbook*. I told him the only piracy charges brought against him would come from the cookbook writer the check and galleys were intended for. Because my friend, in his story, said he used some of the identical recipe titles, such as *Skewered Young Meat and Pounded Raw Mauritanian Moor's Balls*. Since he was so adept in changing the review's name from *New Quarterly* to *New Fortnightly* and the book's title to *The American Gay Cookbook*, I told him I didn't mind the heist myself. What I might mind is if you in a story wrote a scene where a writer tells another writer about his writer friend who's writing a story about a writer and using some of the first writer's experiences in it, such as the one about his having submitted a story to a review and getting back instead of his story and rejection slip, a check and the galleys to a book he didn't write called *The American Gay* or *Gay American Cookbook*. If you did and included the same recipe and my friend's book and literary review titles, you might have to account to them both."

"I'd write the story from the point of view of the writer who's using your experiences and wondering why you haven't asked to see the story he's writing about a writer so you could rip it up."

"*Non non*, not yet, Paul," she later says. "Strange: you comply and die, I live and thrive. I'm repressive and you're receptive. But I'd be hurt if you didn't," and she bumps about till he manages, "Trick I picked up in a how-to marriage manual: you'd be surprised," and leaves.

"Come for cocktails at six," she calls soon after to say.

If he were writing a story which for some reason had a cocktail party in it he'd use Shelly's device if she hadn't used it first of suggesting at the end of whatever was written on the last page he wrote that the reader write his own cocktail party scene on the following blank page as the writer hasn't had an original idea or insight about cocktail parties in years and has kept them out of his own fiction because he thinks they're the most uninteresting gatherings to write and read about and one of the most wearisome to attend. Sitting on a couch at Shelly and Alain's cocktail party he writes what he might put on that blank page.

"Someone came up to me before and said, 'What do you do?'

"Somebody else came up to me and said, 'What's that you're drinking?'

"Somebody came up to me right after that and said, 'What do you do?'

"I'm sitting on a couch near the bar at the Bustelli cocktail party writing down some of what I see, hear, feel and do.

"A lady said to a man 'The olive in my martini is enormous and black. I think the bartender's drunk.'

"'That's Lilian Pilgrim's boy,' the man said, 'didn't you know?'

"'My, he's grown. I thought he was still in high school.'

"'He is.'

"Then what's he doing serving alcohol at a grownup party?'

"'Could be he put that olive in your drink as a joke.'

"I can't go to the can now as this room's packed and I don't want to give up my much-coveted seat.

"A man just came up to me, slapped my shoulder, causing the line you see running down this page, and said, 'Why'd you make that funny squiggly line down your page?'

"A woman came to the party slightly soused and put her cigarette out in the clam dip on my end table.

"I wouldn't include that last sentence in a short story as I don't like cigarettes, clam dips, any mention of them or linkup of the two. Touches like that proving nothing but a writer's smugness or distaste for people and preference for ugly contemporary minutiae, should be shunned.

"I don't know if what I just wrote is valid or if I even believe it, so scratch the last paragraph out.

"The second-to-last paragraph would have to remain unscratched on a blank page of a short story if I were given the chance to write on one, if the paragraphs preceding it are to make any sense.

"I'm not sure if I spelled minutiae right 3 paragraphs above or if I even used the word in its proper sense.

"I'm also not sure if I used the phrase 'proper sense' in its proper sense or if the two words 'proper sense' could be considered a phrase.

"I've a good opportunity of truly expressing myself here and am obviously tossing it oy vey.

"If I had written that last sentence for possible publication I would have looked up the correct spelling for oy vey and italicized the expression as I would all foreign words to distinguish them from identically-spelled but differently-pronounced and -defined English words. I also don't think I would have wasted so many new paragraphs on such simple statements and would have combined this paragraph, for example, and the preceding 7 paragraphs into one.

"While I was counting the above mentioned paragraphs to see if they really did total 8, a woman said to me, 'Who do you belong to, Shelly or Alain?' 'Sharon,' I said. 'Be serious,' she said. 'To be honest rather than serious, I don't know what your question means.' 'To be courteous rather than dishonest,' she said, 'are you part of Alain's New York art world crowd or Shelly's western civilization writers and actors crowd, for you look like you could be from either one.' 'I'm from hunger,' I said. 'That's an old joke,' she said, 'so I know you're not from here.'

"I could have said 'What makes you think I look like I'm from either crowd?' But I think I know what she would've said (pen, eyes, clothes, pad, combativeness, ripostes) and I don't like anyone talking about my mannerisms and looks.

"In my story I'd furnish 2 back-to-back blank pages for the cocktail party scene.

"By the way. I told her 'To be discourteous rather than undishonest I couldn't be,' and I said, 'Shelly.' She said, 'Prosit' and left.

"A man said, 'Why you sitting by yourself in a couch corner next to a clam dip with a cigarette in it writing down what you see, hear, feel and do when you know darn well it won't be worth a whit when you look at it the next minute or whenever when?'

"'Posterity,' I think I said.

"Of all the people in this house I'd like talking to and holding right now: Sharon, but she's asleep. Is that peculiar? Would it be more peculiar to wake her to talk to her and hold her? Even more peculiar: to tell Sharon all that? And perhaps most peculiar of all: to slip this page under her door in an envelope marked For Sharon Only and with this paragraph underlined?

"A man said, 'What do you think of the president's economic message last night?' I said, 'I'm not especially interested in economics or politics.' He said, 'Come come, everyone's interested in politics, as there's practically nothing we do where it doesn't affect our lives. Man's a political animal

Aristotle said and you can hardly quote any truer words than that. 'Quoting them in the original Greek might be truer,' I said. 'And besides, I didn't know Aristotle was referring to politics when he said that, but since I'm not very interested in politics I won't go further into it.' He said, 'What's in your glass: tetrahydracannabinol?' 'Well, that sounds like Greek,' I said. 'And that sounds like a paltry old joke,' he said, 'so I know you're not from around here.' 'Thomas,' a woman said, 'you must meet someone I feel you must meet.' Did she drag him away, fearful of an argument with me? I don't know. It's too late. He's gone now. He was clearly P.O.ed though. Or P O'd. I don't know the right way to write that, though it's probably like KO'd. Or KOed. Or K.Oed. Or

"Shelly said, 'Having fun? Every so often you must give a cocktail party in this village or you're not invited to them. If you're not invited to them then you're ostracized from all the other social affairs and considered uncommunity-minded to boot. It's possible that after that, if your house is on fire and isn't endangering anyone's life or the house or parked car of a social-civic minded neighbor who gives cocktail parties, the community would let it burn. So you could say I give these parties to protect my manuscripts upstairs that I might not be able to rescue and replace in case the village let my house burn down.'

"'To boot or not to boot,' a young man said to her, 'that's a kicker's question. Not quite. But I'm sure if I reflected on the second part of that remark long enough, I'd come up with something related to football or booteries that would elicit a laugh.'

"That was more a retelling in my own words of what Shelly and the young man said before, as I haven't the memory to remember it verbatim or the skill to write down everything they say so fast. Also, the man interjected his sentences after Shelly said the words 'to boot.'

"While I was writing the above paragraph, the young man said something I didn't quite hear about shortstop errors and bootees which everybody around found funny. When I asked him to repeat it he said, 'Catch as catch can or not,' which no matter how much it could seem like it, wasn't the crack he made about the shortstop, and as far as I could tell, has nothing to do with bootees.

"A man came into the room with a sound-movie camera clamped to his shoulder and is filming a short of a cocktail party. He asks people questions. Sits beside me. He's about to speak. No, he adjusts his camera and mike. Turns camera on, holds mike between us. This is what he says.

"'May I ask what youre writing there?'

"'That id have to furnish 3 consecutive blank pages if I was writing a story where I wanted the reader to write in his own cocktail party scene.'

"'Thats what youre writing down now?'

"'what im writing dn now is tht its vry difcult getng all this dn excpt in shorthand, whch i dnt thk il be abl 2 rd bk 2 myslf ltr on.'

"'tht wht u cam 2 th cktl prty 2do?'

"'nt wht I cm 2 th prty 2 do bt smthng I tht of whl I ws at th prty & wch I nw find vry dfclt 2 do & thk ill file awy & mybe try & use in my work as an idea 1 day bt wch wil prbly turn out 2 b unusbl & unworthwhl.'" (*Tht* stands 4 thought, think & that.)

"'i'm sory, I missed tht,' I sy. 'wht ws it u just sd 2 ths man jst now?'

"'i sd,' tha man he spoke 2 sys, 'pepl ought 2 do wht thy wnt 2 do.' for instnc, at cktl prties I lk 2 drnk. u 2 hv 1 wit me?'

"'sure,' I sy. 'sctch on th rks.'

"'i wd if I wasn't makg a mvie. later.'

"'You're not intentionally drawing attention to yourself?' Shelly says to me. 'wht did u jst write down? o god, u wrot "yr nt intentnly drng atnshn 2 yrslf?" whts tht now? No—that. D R N G is drg? And now D R G is dg? im sur yv smthg usfl in mind for it.'

"'Paul,' Alain says, 'lt me introduce u 2 sm pepl. wht? u tht tht worthy 2 wrt down? I dont know. I won't bother you till you ask.'

"'No no, Alain, I'm finished now.' No I'm not. 'No im nt.' A yng woman came into the room. Ill follow her with my pen till she leaves. She walks across th rm 2 th bar, asks brtndr 4 a drink. he pours coke frm a qt bottle. she asks if she cn hv a piece of lemon in her coke. 'Just the juice, not the slice,' she says. A seed from th lmn has aparntly fallen into th glas of cok. Sh sys 'iv always had this fear it might get caught in my throat or appendix. do u hv a spoon 2 tak it out with?' He looks. 'I've a swizzle stic,' he sys. They try. she 1st, thn th brtndr. 'The seed keeps sliding off just as we get it going up the glass,' brtndr sys. A young man comes over. 'I—er—wht r u doing, Raina?' he sys. sh sys—she looks distraught. th lmn seed jst fel off th stic agn. sh sys—sh scratches her 4head. 'if u hadn't sudnly frightened me I cdve had it up. he—the brtndr—whts yr nam agn, pleez?' 'Jack,' brtndr sys. 'Jac dropd a lmn seed into my coke whn he was squzing the lmn into th glas & I alwys thk it cd get caught in my appndx & caus appendicitis, so im trying 2 get it out.' 'thts an old wives tale,' her friend sys. sh sys 'maybe the Fox & th Grapes is an old w's tale, but yul cm visit me in th hosptl 2 tel me th lmn seed was also a tale if I hv 2 hv my apndx out bcaus of it?' 'that's a fable tht fox wit th cropped ears or whtevr u sd th tale was wit th grapes. but wdnt it b easier getng th seed out wit a spoon?' 'i only hv a swizl stic'

jac sys, '& we tried.' yng man—'th kitchen.' Raina—
'for a spoon?' ym—'thy must hv 1 there.' Raina—'of
cours thy hv thm ther. but wdnt it b simplr 2 pour
anthr glas of cok rathr thn trubl th hosts?' ym—'y
shd it b any trubl?' jac—'ill gladly giv u anthr cok if u
want, miss.' 'yes' sh sys. 'u wnt 1 thn?' jac sys. 'yes' sh
sys. 'ill hv a bourbon on cubes' ym sys. '1 brbn ovr ice'
jac sys. '& a litl water in ther' ym sys. 'this enuf?' jc
sys. 'enuf!' 'no lmn in my coke this time pleez' raina
sys. 'il be xceptnly carefl wit this 1' j sys. 'no matter
how crfly someon mt try & b in squzng it' ym sys,
'smtimes a seed can fall unvoidbly out of a lmn into
th glas &—&—1 time faced with—same dilema.' th
ym had a hanky over his mouth so I cdnt completely
undrstdnd him. but raina sd 2 hm 'wht hapend?' 'wht
hapnd?' he sd. 'wel th seed fel into th glas of course.'
'i know' sh sd, 'but were u abl 2 get it out?' 'I don't
hv any phobias' th ym says 'or any lik thos u mt hv,
so i didn't care whether i swalowd that seed or not.
it digests anyway, or passes thru.' 'not alwys' R sys.
'wht about a lemon peel?' jac sys. 'wht abt a lmn pl?'
R sys. 'I mean ill put it in yr coke if u want. theyre
precut, no seeds attached & contain th essence of th
lmn, wch I thk wd mk thm as strng as th lm slice sqzd
ovr th cok.' 'no, im stil afrd' sh sys. 'thn i cd jst ring yr
glas rim wit th lm pl' j sys. 'stil' sh sys, 'tho it is vry
sweet of u 2 ask.' 'how bout us going outsid?' th ym
sys 2 her. 'it is a nice nite' sh sys. 'its alrite' ym sys. 'r
all these pple here yr familys friends?' sh sys. 'som r
reltives' ym sys. 'Dumb broad,' Jack says after they're
gone. Looking at me, thinking I heard, he seems
embarrassed. 'Want a refill?' he says. 'Everybody
seems 2 hv stopped drinking & im hired till 12.'

"Before I get up to give him my glass, I'll
fold up the papers I've written on and put them in
my pocket. Probly 5 blank pp I'd need for that story,

maybe 6.

"We're counting on your helping us with Sharon's birthday party tomorrow," Shelly says to him as he leaves. "Goodnight. Sweet dreams. Thanks for coming, Paul."

He walks to the point. When he was here two winters ago he wrote a short story about a writer who came to a similar village to get over a woman in New York who had stopped seeing him. In the story and real life she was an actress portraying an actress on a daytime television soap opera who was in love with a writer of soap operas who couldn't give up his wife for her. One night, in the story and real life, she told Paul she couldn't see him anymore as she was in love with and thinks she'll be marrying the actor who plays the writer on the show. In the story and real life he had to sit down for fear of falling down and she said he was beginning to act like one of the more unconvincing morose characters on her soap. "The writer you're in love with?" he said and she said Abe would never act so callow and doleful in real life or on the show. She asked him to leave and he said not yet. "Do I have to call the police?" and he said "Please let's just go to bed one last time and I swear I'll go." Both in real life and the story she said, "You've got to be crazier than I first thought you were when I met you and later disbelieved." He slapped her face, pushed her into her bedroom and told her to take off her clothes. In the story he had to pin her arms down and sit on her while he removed her clothes. In real life he didn't pin her down and she took off her clothes while she sat on the edge of the bed. In the story and in real life she said if he was so intent on raping her as he seemed to be, then she wasn't going to stop him. As she'd been warned by friends and in a recent women's magazine article that she could damage her vagina that way. "Irreparably sometimes," she said in real life. He doesn't remember using that last line in the story, because he thinks he felt it would have sounded too banal to be believed. Now he'd use it, if he already hadn't, and he makes a note in his scratch pad to add that line to the story if the line he might have written in place of it isn't a better one and if this line can intelligibly be put in. Both in real life and the story she again pleaded with him to leave and he said he couldn't. When she cried because she was scared of the bodily harm he might do her in bed and later, out of self-reproach, when he was through, he broke down, in real life, said he must have been temporarily insane to have threatened her like that, and left. In the story he held her down, got on top of her and tried making love. She said something like "As I said before, Perry. You don't have to force me, as I'm not about to fight. I can see you're fixed on raping me, so I don't want to risk rupturing my vaginal walls and maybe as a result restrict my childbearingness and facility for making love unrestrainedly with other men." The act was physically difficult and painful for them both. In real life, a month before that night, she would have said "It's sleeping, Paul, let's wait." In the story she later said that rape or whatever he wanted to call it, it could have been pleasurable for her if he were the man she was in love with but for her own reasons didn't want to make love tonight while he most demonstrably did, or if she was even in some small way still attracted to him. "But I'm not. In every way you're unattractive to me, no more now than before." He said he could make her attracted to him and she said that was only the insufferable hubris speaking in him again. He said hubris was one of a dozen words he'd looked up at least 20 times in the last ten years and would still have to look up again when he got home tonight. In the story he looked up the word when he got home and gave the definition. In real life now he doesn't know what the word means and writes hubris down on his scratch pad and asterisks it. In the story and real life he made a late evening call to her from the phone booth on this point a week after he left her apartment. In the story and real life he said something like "I'm calling from this point which is on an icy peninsula a mile out to sea and where I can hear the sounds of buoys, gulls, waves, bells, fishing boat motors from nearby and far off, the clinging and pinging of the halyard against the flagpole at the point's tip, and somehow it's the maddest and saddest and happiest and sappiest and yet sanest phone call I've ever made. For you see I'm both speaking to you while at the same time so totally alone and now being covered like everything else out here including the mouthpiece and coin slots and telephone wires and poles with snow." In the story she said "I hope you get buried to death and die, goodbye," and hung up. In real life she said he sounds awful and there's nothing she can do for him and hung up.

He phones Storm and says "I'm phoning from that peninsula point phone I last phoned you from and which I never would have done if it wasn't around the same time at night and so soon after seeing some of the same people and the same sea and shore sounds couldn't be heard and the point wasn't just as deserted as it was when I phoned you in what in a few fall months will be two winters ago."

"If it's snowing," she says, "I hope you get buried to death and die, goodbye."

"And if it's raining or let's say the meteors are showering as they're now but weren't then showering? Or the sun's thundering and mountains are lightninging and stars and moon are closing in and earth's fissuring and oceans are tidalwaving and this village and your city and our country and countries and continents are disappearing worldwide? Day the earth ended—a timetown title for a short story, but a workable theme for one I'd work on if I hadn't used it twice before. Remember the husband-and-wife archeological team? The last two people on earth who seek shelter in the cave they've been exhuming for years. And just as the cave's crumbling they discover an intact skull and frame and enfaced slate and stylus that are probably a million years older than the oldest bones and writing materials ever found of protohuman American, and also the skeleton's digging and cooking utensils that are very much like their own. And what about old Philly Worstwords who's awakened from a series of dreams of the successive loves of his youth and artistic successes of his middle age to find his top floor apartment walls collapsing and all the surrounding buildings and blocks plummeting. And from that hospital bed in his now towering wall-less single room, observing the dissolution of his neighborhood and then the entire city and countrywide beyond. 'Why me?' he kept asking—remember that, Storm? 'Why me, why me, why me?'"

In the studio he dials the California phone number Rose sent him last week when she wrote that she and Lucia had finally found an interim home. In the letter she also said they'd be driving east for a vacation in a few weeks and was Pennsylvania before or after New York? He hasn't seen them in three years. He wrote about that last afternoon with them in a story that opens with Rose saying she's pregnant by him though she was living with her husband at the time, and closes more than two years later with Rose and Lucia in their Volvo entering a San Francisco freeway on their way back to L.A., though in real life

the cities were the other way around as he wanted
that story to end with the letter A because he began it
with the woman's name Zee. Nobody ever noted that
alphabetic artifice or the 24 others he planted in that
story, as they haven't in his story where all the men
have names that could be women's, such as Robin and
Dale. Or in another story where all the city names
start off with Saint, San or Santa and the women
are named after ores, alloys, metals, gems and semi-
precious stones.

"Rose is on the property but three miles
through the woods from here," a man says. "This long
distance? Give us your number and we'll have her call
you back on our magic telephone."

Last commune she lived on was vegetarian,
Rose wrote, and so authoritarian that when they found
her and five-year-old Lucia sharing a beef jerky, they
forced Rose to eat six bowls of cold porridge made
from organically-grown hand-ground oats and Lucia
three. Lucia became so hysterical after the third bowl
that she had to be injected with tranquilizers and both
were evicted the next day. Always mistakes, Rose
wrote in another letter, all but the last he's included in
an epistolary story composed solely of edited versions
of the letters she's sent him over the past five years,
with all the people's names switched around and the
same dates and locations other than the exact streets
and RFD and box numbers reproduced.

This year she fell in love with a junkie she said
in the letter and story, and the year before that with an
alcoholic, and she hoped both would say, "Ah, at last
a woman who turns me on, someone to communicate
with, to *be* with, now I can throw away my junk, my
gin, my jive, forget my literary critiques and satirical
cartoons and go off with her and start a farm and do
something worthwhile." One man she recently met

at a psychodrama, which is the incident he ended the story with. "Everybody was putting him down. So I stood up and said to him, 'What you really want and need most is to mount a woman and ram and jam it all the way in there, am I right?' Everyone hooted at me, but the man said, 'Lady, you knocked the nose on the head. But no chick will let me do it because they think I'm either too horny or homely or both.' 'Well, first let's end this pressing need you have and after that we can get down to the weightier problem of why you think you're homely or have to be horny, but not in front of these unfeeling creeps.' The rest of the psychodrama participants began beating up on me when I refused to be mounted in front of them. When the man tried tearing them off me, they broke a few of his teeth. They only let us go after they had ripped, bit, scratched and clawed most of our clothes off and some of our hair and skin, and later we went to bed. He turned out to be leery, a weirdy, a bad lover and born loser, I think syphilitic and infanticidal, maybe even sapropelic and homosexual, certainly sadistic, sodomitic, satanic, scabietic, scrofulous, carious, dyshidrosic, dyspeptic, the worst. Mistakes. Always mistakes..."

On a TV talk show is a writer who once held the same university writing fellowship the year Paul did. The comedian, who's the regular host's replacement, says, "Ooooh, what big words you use, grampa. Better to chew us out with I reckon, though how do you expect us to know what you're saying?"

The writer's attacking the President, Congress, marriage, religion, education, writing fellowships, whites—"All whites, including me. I'm attacking myself."

"Now there's a switcheroo for this show," the comedian says. "Usually it's love me, worship me, adore me, yum yum yum. And fine with me what you say, so long as you next don't start knocking comedians."

"Only white ones."

"Since that encompasses most of the comedians who get the best show spots and club dates and make the most money and excludes some of my very able black comedian friends, then I agree with that. Or I concur with that. I don't know. For you see, deep down underneath I'm yellow. Though I'm not sure the audience agrees with you."

Lots of boos and noes from the audience.

"They the people speak," the comedian says.

"The people here are all white."

"Noooo," the audience says.

"Then you're mostly white," the writer says. "I heard a few yeses and applause before, but they were roundly drowned out by the bellicose white noes."

"Noooo."

"The noes know," the comedian says.

"The noes know what? That they're a sounder of obtuse snorting slobbish swines? The noes know their noses. Led. You're all penned, eat garbage and are led."

"Noooo."

"You have no direction, no meaning to your lives. Which is why you come to this dumb show to see this white—excuse me—yellow comedian and white writer, and you're not even aware of it. You're ruining this country, do you know that?"

"Noooo."

"Polluting and pesticiding it, overpopulating and depleting it. Killing it and millions of old and young innocents in Asiatic lands. This comedian's siblings."

"Noooo," though there are some cheers and

laughs.

"You mean yessss. Yes, that you're despoiling this land. Yes, that you're debauching its precious language—the most significant legacy we have to pass along and which you've let be abused and distorted so the fascistic masters can lead and use you for their demented ends, and also other cultures and their best people, languages and lands. Just see if I'm wrong."

"You're wrongggg."

"Indian assassins. Black and brown genociders. And me too. I'm to blame too. But wait and see when the real fascists come. The prepotent ones who created you to set the political and emotional backdrop for this country so they can really take over and wipe out all the Chicanos and PR's and street people and radicalized workers and students and apostatized profs. Then you'll have what you suicidal bigots wanted all along. And that's a right-wing totalitarian government that will make this country unendurable for anyone but the white-on-white white reactionaries, which is going to eventually knock off this beautiful world, take my word."

"You agree with that, audience?"

"Noooo."

"White fascist know-nothing nose-ringed no-account swines."

"Who does agree with you?" the comedian says. "I'm not trying to be facetious or anything. Meaning, I would if it could get me a laugh—but who do you like?"

"Sensitive, outspoken, courageous, vigorous lusty lyrical ethical anti-autocratic revolutionary individuals who aren't cattle, sheep or swines."

"But before you had several kind words for cattle. If memory serves me right, you said you only wished we had the minds of bovines instead of—"

"People who aren't obsequious toadying bootlicking pigeons."

"Pigeons now. And toads. I think you maybe just got a thing against all animals."

"Pigeons who'll wind up being the patsies for Washington and Wall Street bunkomen turned latter-day *führers* and superpatriotic despot pigs."

"Hitler was on Wall Street? I mean, I know he was a pretty sloppy housepainter and kind of a jerk— say. Remember that witty ditty during War Two? 'Whistle while you work. Mussolini'—I could never hold a tune, but 'Mussolini, is a meanie, Hitler is a stockbroker.' But all kidding aside. No, honestly folks, because I want to have a serious conversation with this guy. Does the F.B.I. know about Herr Schickelgruber's pre-war blue chip investments and selling long in short pants?"

"People who don't feel the need for jumbo jets and twelve-lane pikes and thousand-dollar stereos and stroboscopic dishwashers and tape decks and back-seat TV sets and air conditioners in their cars."

"What's wrong with an air conditioner in your car?"

"Noooo," the audience says.

"Yeah. Cross my heart and hope to plotz. Keeps me cool on those hot New York days. After all, you don't want me driving my oofy in-laws around town with damp sticky odor-filled you-know-whats, do you?

"Yessss."

"You do? Say, this *is* a freaky audience tonight. Where we doing this show from, 42nd Street? No, that's not nice. I mean, you are freaky, but there are a lot of good compassionate people molesting and murdering muggers on 42nd Street."

"Can you smell new-mown grass in an air-conditioned car?"

"On 42nd Street?"

"In the country. Because at least one out of every two cars I see on the road today has its windows up and the riders can't hear or smell a thing outside. They're also probably freezing their ------ ------ off with those machines."

"Those two beeps you heard just now weren't from any clown's nose, folks. No, sir."

"See what fools they are. All I have to do is mumble one overused Anglo-Saxon curse word like ------ and they laugh till their tummies and tiddies ache. Oh you ------ ------."

"Noooo."

"Listen," the comedian says. "Hold it down a minute, folks, I've got something important to say. Now listen. I'm not against controversy. Ratings supposedly soar when the show becomes controversial, and I also can't deny that off the air I might use a few naughty words myself from time to time. Well, it's true. But there is such an organization known as the F.C.C. And though I don't know what those initials stand for. And after my confession about naughty words, I don't think that august body would enjoy my haphazarding an essentially nightclub comedian's guess. I do know that it doesn't tolerate vulgarity on the air, and it could even be a little offensive for the children in the audience and at home when they should be in bed. So go to sleep, children at home. And you small fry in the audience—put your ears over your hands or in your pockets, but don't you listen, okay? Because we don't want to be beeped till we're bumped off the air."

"Now see, that I find intolerable."

"Not only that, it could reduce my income."

"Not your getting bumped off the air. But saying, 'Don't listen' to the one age group that most compellingly needs to hear the truth about the frauds and fakeries of the present social order and its hypocritical institutions that guide, teach and preach to them if they're ever to revolt, and not just spiritually, and really fight to make this world, and I mean for everyone, an equitable nonprivileged unexploited and unalienated place for people to breathe, think, grow, crow, create, procreate, live, long, lust, love, work and die in."

"Okay. Strong views, this man, and a command of the English language—whew! you don't have to know what he's saying, but just listening to him is a treat. Now what do you say we talk about a more harmless subject. Literature, for instance. Something I know a lot more about."

"All writers should hock their typewriters and join the masses in the street."

"Masses of what?"

"This is horrendous," and he gets up and leaves the stage.

"Where'd he go? Hey, Mal, where you going? God, that guy walks fast. Come on back, will ya, and let's be friends. Then let's have a walking race. Then we'll just stare at each other while the announcer reads sonnets. And you didn't sing that old sea ballad you promised. Sure, you can go. Made a mint with his last two novels—not that I'm knocking it. It's the international way, *comprendo*? *Nicht so*? But me? Walk off once like him and that, my friends, would be show business as they say—forever. And bestsellers I don't write. Some people will even say I can't write and there won't be many who will take issue with them. Because anybody here read my last book? Come on, don't be ashamed. Stand up if your belt and garters are on tight. Well, let's not all rise at once. Anybody even remember the title? What was that? Be brave

and shout it out. No, it wasn't *Gone With the Wind*,
but thanks, Mom. Huh? No, not *Madame Bovary*
either—but Flaubert, right? And you people thought
I never went to college. *Crime and Punishment*? That's
what the readers thought I inflicted on them. *War and
Peace*? An apt description of what went on between
the editors and me perhaps. It was...*Madame Bovary
Returns* the hopeful horticulturist in the front row
says. We're all quipsters here. No, I said horticulturist.
That's a hearts-and-flowers man with brains. *Swann's*
what? Never heard of it. *Oedipus Sex*? Never saw it.
Be a Wolf? Who even wrote it? And is that a nice
thing to advise a married man? *Dead Souls*?—you said
it, brother, not me—is what I think I have in devoted
readers here. *The Trial*? What this guessing game's
getting to become. But *Wild Walter's World*. There it
is. My autobiog. Born with a silver spoon and golden
locks in my mouth, which is why I talk this way. My
mom never took them out because she thought they
might improve my face. Someone once suggested our
retitling it to *Crazy Publisher's Catastrophe*, because you
know what that book sold? How many fingers you got
on your hand? Not you. Our orchestra chief just held
up six fingers on his right hand and seven on his left—
but the lead fiddler next to you. The one who got his
hand caught in some thigamagig like that stereoscopic
dish conditioner our writer friend mentioned and
had to have a few fingers removed. Well, his hand.
Only the one that was operated on. Count how many
fingers he's got left. Subtract two. That's how many
copies of my book sold. I still got it home. Under a
broken kitchen chair leg. In the same brown paper bag
they sold it to me in. My wife didn't want it on the
bookshelf because we already had a book there. And
our daughter refused to sit on it to reach the dinner
table and the mutt still thinks it's the oddest looking

fire hydrant around. Truthfully, it sold pretty well and in more languages than I knew existed. And starting this month, any one of you out there can be one of its two million paperback owners. *Wild Walter's World.* I said the title too low? That was *Wild Walter's World,* folks. Not *Wild Walter's World Folks,* but just *Wild Walter's World.* Okay. Now, our guest really left? He's not back there? Daphne, you looked? Nobody? Dashed out of the studio with our library prop and ordered his chauffeur to drive him straight home? Well, this is a very intellectual show tonight. But before introducing our next eminent author—and it beats me how we're going to carry out our literary discussion format if it's now just going to be me and him here. Or I. All these brilliant writers around the place are making me unsure with the language. Maybe we could bring up some members of the audience to join in the discussion. They'd like that, right? Yeahhh. Anyway, before all that, time for plugs. Have you always had a deep-seated yearning to write great novels and story articles and lead the happy enriching life of a successful author, but everyone said you had to have a big name or your work would never sell? Well, the Westport Famous Writers Correspondence School— I'm joshing. But this all-but-indescribable product I have here and which is really something to write home about, folks, as it can literally do the magical cleaning work of a thousand-and-one genies..."

"Paul?"

"Hey, Rose, how are you?"

"Fine thank you how are you?"

"And Lucia?"

"Fine. Family's doing fine? You know I'm untalkative on the phone. What do you want?"

"Um glum—to hear you say you're untalkative on the phone?"

"Very untalkative on the phone."

"Lots of untalkatives on the phone."

"Can't we stop with the untalkatives on the phone?"

"To find out if you're still writing your journals?"

"Daily. I was in fact logging today's account when they said you wanted me to call back, which I also wrote down. And now, as I'm talking to you, I'm trying to transcribe everything you said before, as this is an unusual event. So far I've the journal question, your double untalkatives on the phone. 'Um bum' and 'And Lucia?' and "Hey, Rose, how are you?' Verbal equivocal and punning around in your work, Paul. Despite everything I've done and might do in my life, do you think I'll post-Rosey be known wholly as Lucia's Madonna and your occasional chronicler and letter recipient and one-time mistress as Milena now is? But we're starving and haven't any food and neither does the main house, so we have to drive down the mountain to the supermarket. Lucia wants to speak to you too."

"I don't think I'm prepared."

"You need a script? It's all right—she doesn't know who you are yet. And unlike me, she likes to speak to anyone who calls. Here."

"But I've never really spoken to her before. Help me if it gets uncomfortably foundered on my part or it's obvious she isn't enjoying the talk because she senses I'm forcing it but she's too well brought up or just doesn't know what to say to cut it off so's letting me falter on."

"Could you please repeat that for my journal jottings starting from 'to her before'?"

"Hello?" a girl says.

"You speak?" Paul says.

"I speak. Lucia speaks."

"You wouldn't remember me, Lucia. I'm Paul. Did you about a month ago get a postcard from a person named Paul?"

"Postcard?"

"Do you know what a postcard is?"

"He says postcard," she says away from the phone.

"Tell him they're neither made from recycled paper nor nourishing."

"Lucia, did you ever get a postcard over the phone?"

"I know a postcard," she says.

"Good. Because you see, I'm a long ways away. So far away from you that if you got on a plane to fly to the city I'm in, the plane would have to fly in the air for many hours to get here. And the postcard takes days and days to get to you also, so to speed things up I'm going to send you one over the phone instead. Do you understand?"

"Yes."

"Fine, then, here goes. A postcard for Lucia over the phone. Dear Lucia. That's your name, right?"

"Dear Lucia Maria Lorn."

"Good. Dear Lucia Maria Lorn. I'm sending you a postcard from a place far away that takes many hours to fly in the air to and I hope you like getting my postcard very much. Love, your friend, Paul."

"What?"

"I just sent you a postcard over the phone. There's not much room on a postcard to write on so I had to make what I said short."

"He's sending a postcard over the phone."

"Lucia, how old are you?"

"Five."

"Five. I see. Do you like to go swimming?"

"What?"

"Swimming. Do you like to run through the forests with the animals?"

"Are no animals here."

"No wild weather-wise animals like woody woodchucks in the woods?"

"No."

"Skunks, chipmunks?"

"No."

"No raccoons, baboons?"

"No."

"Moose, goose? Grouse, mouse? Cockatoos, kangaroos? Chickadees, wallabies?"

"No no no no."

"Well, then, do you like to fly high in the sky with a magpie and other birds?"

"Are no birds here."

"Do you like to swim in the ocean with the fish?"

"No fish."

"Sure there are fish."

"He says there're fish here."

"In the ocean, I said. I don't mean in fishbowls and tanks. And you're near the ocean. I know where La Honda is. I used to live around there. And you and your mom and I once built a whopping big bonfire on the beach nearby that burned through the night, but that was too far back for you to remember."

"I remember."

"You remember the mickeys we roasted? The wieners as big as big bed pillows we toasted?"

"We have to go get some food now."

"If you're going now then I'll write a real postcard with stamps, as the other one I only read you on the phone."

"Someone else."

"We have a ride down for food now, Paul."

"She speaks, does she read?"

"Only the words *flash* and *cards* on the giant flash cards I hold up. *Giant* she only knows by my accompanying drawing of one and *I* she thinks is a bed on its headboard, and the reading set doesn't have a card for *hold up*."

"I also wanted to know when you're driving east."

"To...know...when...I'm...driving...east. Got you. To that I say 'I don't know if I am.' I don't know if I am, Paul. I...don't...know..."

"You can stay with me. I've a new apartment right around the block from my folks that'll be ready in two days."

"In the unlikelihood that I even start out from California and get past my friends in Pennsylvania, I'll stay with you if I don't get stuck in New Jersey, yes."

"If I flew out tomorrow on a 27-day excursion flight, would I be able to stay with you?"

"My camper's too small for us all."

"No attachable sleeping bags or available space in the main house?"

"If he...means...he...and I...then I...tell him..."

"Stop that."

"I'm with someone else."

"No one else. You and I. Someone else you can always be with. You and me. Woman and man. Man on woman, woman on man. Side by side, grunt to grunt, stomach to stem, my woman, my man."

"To fall in love?"

"We'll see. But just to be with me."

"For two weeks?"

"Three. Past the excursion flight mini maximum into the unknown beyond. I don't know.

That's the unknown. I don't know if that's the unknown. What do I know? What I knew? What I know now? That's it, no. Even what I knew as the well-known turns out to be unknown again and again. What I know is that I can't say I don't know anything, as that's not implicit in my saying I don't. Nah, maybe not even that. But you're with someone else. A man?"

"He is. I am. Quote he is, I am, unquote. I'm sorry. It's exhausting enough chattering this stuff over the phone. And my despicable compulsion to write everything down simply because I began doing it when I was six. For you I'll tear up this journal page. Book 83, page 122, lines nine through eighteen. I tore it up. Eliot's piaculative and I'm not sure about Pound's, but now mine. Did you hear the tear, the tears? There's a lit fireplace a hand's toss away from here and the expiatory ultimate would be for me to throw in my hands. The penultimate would be this entire journal's death fire. Naturally not my other 82 books, as throwing them in has no estimable sacrificial grading and is less likely to occur than self-immolation and I'd also sear my arms pulling them out as Nora with *Stephen's Arsonist* did, and then I couldn't drive. And Lucia can't both reach the floor clutch and steer. And we've got to go. I hate belaboring the point, but the all-night supermarkets in the county don't stay open all night. There was a suit to that effect and the county court rules that 'all-night' means only till midnight. The stores could stay open past then if they liked, but they couldn't put 'all-morning' on their signs unless they meant to stay open till noon from twelve or one on. Goodbye."

"Don't go."

The second author is on the television studio stage with a panel made up from the audience. One person's saying to him "You mean each graffiti to you—"

"Graffito," the writer says.

"Each graffito to you is the lowest form of writing."

"The highest. Because in spite of it being the oldest creative writing extant, it still manages to be fresher and more succinct than an aphorism. More honest than a dictum. More intelligible and less pompous than most poetry, fiction and drama. Fairier than a fairy tale. Smuttier than any pornography. And more fervid, shocking, laughable, suggestive and stimulating than any apothegm, elegy, epopee, idyll, rondel, proverb or motto. Perhaps only a last will and testament is more suspenseful, rewarding and upsetting, and only then to the prospective beneficiaries and resultant heritors and those persons cut out. An epithalamium and love letter more pleasure-giving. And a suicide note or cenotaph inscription with its attending prayer for the dead from the prayer book more able to move us. Though what we always have to take into account there is the pre-established emotional aura enveloping all those compositions, which is kind of weighing it a bit in their favor, wouldn't you say?"

"You forgot the draft notice," the comedian says.

"And 'The Army regrets to inform you' and military discharge papers and prison release writ. And a foreclosure notice and poison-pen letter or help message written in blood or strippled in snow or desert sand. Or skywriting to a kid. The first acceptance check to an essayist. Or runes, cuneiform or epigraphs to a paleographer or epigraphist. Or a revolutionary manifesto, pronuncimento, passport, report card, diploma, dope sheet, apostolic brief, search warrant, birth announcement, marriage license, biopsy report, divorce papers, death decree, play review, rare signature, initial shingle, pink slip, black list, blue ribbon, white paper, red-penciling, yellow journalism, urinated namewriting, ardent bark incising or the electric bulb bulletins around the old New York Times building saying 'Stock market crash' or 'President's dead' or 'War's over' or 'declared.' But none touch on so many varied emotions or is so consistently unboring and diverting though not electrifying as those dirty little words, scrawlings and invitations on washroom walls."

"One final question I have," a panel member says, "is how do you find the time to write all your novels? Now when I even have to make out a grocery list—"

"Time's there, it's where you use it. Now this might seem paradoxical, but whenever a book's aching to get out of me, I fly to Las Vegas, register at its most opulent hotel and do a first draft in almost a single sitting. Because with all those free shows, booze, card tables, women and bookmakers around, there are too many temptations to leave my room. When my work's finished, I ride back to the airport, drop a few hundred half dollars in the slot machines till my plane arrives, and fly home without ever stepping into a casino or cathouse."

The comedian holds up a six-pack of diet soda. "Here's one item you'll never have to gamble your weight on."

"Copywriter," the writer says.

"It helps pay my library overdues."

"Paul," Shelly whispers, turning off the TV. "You genuinely asleep?"

"Does Alain know about us?"

"Do you ever read the food labels on pickle jars

and packaged bread? If you do, what's polysorbate-80 and pyridoxine hydrochloride and what do they do to you, not the food? You might suspect the usefulness of these strange-sounding additives, but if you like the product and don't want to make it yourself, you'll continue to buy and eat it, trust that its manufacturer wouldn't do anything that criminal or careless to jeopardize his good name and sacrifice his business, and not read that sedulously the same label again, unless it says in capital letters 'Warning, this product might be hazardous to your health,' which approaches Alain's attitude towards us."

"You're saying he knows?"

"If he does, I don't think he cares. If he does care, I don't think he'll do anything about it. If he does anything about it, I don't think it will be much. At the most he might get disturbed with himself, think that whatever he'd do or say would be wrong or embarrassing, think that he might more accurately be misjudging or overstating the situation, but it will have little to do with us if we continue to behave discreetly and by all exterior appearances remain his unalarming house guest and affectionate and faithful writer-housewife. So we're in the clear as so far all the propionates are."

Next morning Paul resumes his short story. Artur and Pete were driving to the stationery store to pick Sylvia up. In the car Artur asked, "Are you sleeping with my wife?"

"Sylvia?"

"Do I have two?"

"But it's absurd."

"Why absurd? Because of her distasteful looks, bearing, physique, carriage, older age, vapid intelligence, minuscule talent, good-naturedness and wit? That I asked when you think I shouldn't or thought I wouldn't or couldn't seems absurd?"

"She's beautiful, adorable, big-hearted, little
of her not to want any part of, etcetera, *et sequential,*
lovely figure, very sexy, biennially she gives me
the hots and throes but this is an in-between year
and last time was while looking at her dusty dust
jacket on the remaindered counter of a block-long
bookstore. And she's bright, witty, prankish, gracious,
also endless termless *ad infinitum, semper eadem, ora
a sempre, semper et ubique, fidelis* and *paratus,* yuh
lucky *hund, und, naturellement,* sempiternally *sempliche
y nulli secundus et e pluribus unum, Herr Zugsfierer,
ich melde gehorsammst, so wus is de mier? enn thaet thi*
gospel sooth. And old? Not old. What a booby boy
idea. But ohh, I love her, and though never thought
of making love to her, since we're only very tight
buddies and professional kinsmen to the end. The
literary Corsican Boys who never tire of talking of
talking and writing and writers, volumes, books,
sections, passages, pages, paragraphs, lines, words,
letters, roots, moots, foots, phonemes, morphemes,
punctuation, syllabication, titles, fascicles, grammar,
drama, polyglot, gollyplot and read each other's
writing and supply what we think is straight honest
advice and approval and Lilliputian to gargantuan
taps, raps, knocks, socks and slams. But—oops, careful,
you're crossing the double white a mite—if you said
you didn't mind our making love and for your own
whims and unconventionalities even encouraged us,
then it might only make a different story, since I
don't think Sylvia and I would want to run the risk
of ruining the rare novel relationship we now have.
Anyway, it's all got to be partially changed after what
you said to me today, because I'll no doubt insert it
in the story I'm presently writing about Sylvia that
has the rest of us represented as minor characters and

which takes place in a fictionalized here and now and now in this same sports car here on an analogous road. And there's always a 50 percent chance that whatever I'm writing will be completed, and then a 15 percent chance that whatever I complete will be published, and if it is, a 95 to 99 percent chance Sylvia will read it. And then I'd predict a 20 to 40 percent chance she'll say to me 'Well, as long as Art's preconvinced about us and you've no objections, we might as well have a go at it once and see what develops. Because even if there's maybe a 50-50 chance we'll like it together and that it will improve our friendship a snatch, and a 10 to 80 percent chance we'll want to do it again and then a 60 to 90 percent chance we'll have the opportunity to and a 30 to 70 percent chance we'll make use of it, I don't think there's a chance in the world we'll ever stop being the close helpful mostly far apart and infrequently-seen and -heard-from friends we now are."

"Bullshit. Get out of the car."

"Only if you stop it first."

"Find your way back, get your clothes, phone for a cab to the ferry and have them bill both fares to me, but leave."

"By the way, Artur."

"No by the ways."

"Then *dit-donc*, Artur, but what you asked about Sylvia and me before isn't half as absurd as your demanding I go."

"*Melodrame*, no less," and he drove off.

"Sob story! Cliff hanger! Palimpsest! Takeoff!" Pete hitched a ride to the house, packed, Sylvia called after he'd phoned for a cab.

"Artur swears he's sorry and would you for Jesus sake please stay? To make up for his confessed foolishness he'll cook us all a princely French peasant

dinner tonight and break open the wine he's been
saving for our tenth anniversary and champagne for
our 25th , if you'll only promise not to have published
for five years what you write about today's incident
and never show any sign to him that you recall what
he said. Why'd you goad him into asking such a
question?"

"And the Golden Georgia Corn for your 50th ?"

"He'd never ask it on his own. He's not
doublefaced or standarded and knows I must know
he has his own piddling girls when he's in the city
alone. These silly slim twinkling saccharine airline
philistines whom he takes to funny places like La
Fondle des Balls where they eat candle drippings and
sip cork nubbins and admire the passing planes they
think are passing stars. And if you stay I promise to
be especially nice to you, Marta won't lecture me for
losing you, and Artur will never propose that question
again."

"Does he in fact know about us?"

"Have you lately read the ingredients lists
on packaged food labels and wondered what's
polysorbate-80 and sodium propionate and
hydraheaded chloride or whatever that preservative or
additive is?"

"You up?" Shelly says on the phone. "Because
last night you did drunkenly pledge to help us
organize Sharon's birthday party today. It'll be good
your getting with children again. For it's unwise for a
writer to lose that total age perspective and miss the
wily sinless sayings prissy misses can so often say."

The housekeeper at their house says, "Mrs.
Bustelli's working and never's to be disturbed cept for
tragedy for twelve."

Alain's with his summer secretary, dictating
letters and grams, checking receipts, inquiries, bills

of lading, sending off prospectuses and parcels and waiting for phone calls from Surakarta, Zaragossa, Bratislava, Lebanon, Rome, Bern. "Good morning. Shelly's seminating in the next room but allows for outside moments from special outsiders. Thanks for your great aid today, Paul" and to his secretary "Was that 'The Modigliani piece you asked for in answer to our London *Times* ad?'"

"'The Modigliani granite caryatid.' We were about to check the index cards for its description, price and profile."

"'Brancusi...Cellini...Ghiberti...15th century anonymous Swabian...Sir Jacob Epstein.' Shouldn't he be under E and if under S, ahead of the Swabian but after Modigliani and maybe even Moore?"

Shelly's propped up in bed, typewriter, papers and manuscript on the writing table across her lap, in her pajamas, Franklin bifocals, bathrobe, *dictionaire*, gossip tea. "Sharon's ready get set. Here's ten dollars. You don't know how grateful. If it's insufficient, she conceals more."

Sharon and friend sit in the back seat of his bus while he drives to the party cake store.

"The middle seat's out so the Multimal can sleep inside," Sharon tells Milly. "You ever going to build him that bed, Paul?"

"Who's the Multimal?" Milly says.

"Just a fabulous creature. Has four noses and six teeth. Can do anything, look like any animal. He's now at Paul's mom's house waiting for a fifth tail to be put on, as he needs five to fly."

"He actually returned to the hospital," Paul says. "Then telephoned me today saying he got sick of the slipshod treatment there again, so he fastened a mop to his four tails and escaped through a window. But he couldn't fly with just four and a mop. He began to drop. And falling so fast from 45 floors high, for the first time in his life he got freaked and blacked out."

"You see," Sharon says, "the Multimal can change to any color and design he likes, so he became black."

"But black on black in black. Like a chunk of coal in a pitch black cave is black. Black like that. Black like the shadow of a black tree on a moonless starless night if someone suddenly threw open a door and cast light is black. So he became light as a shadow by being black and floated the last few feet to the ground safe and sound. Then he changed to the color green, because he was feeling upset from the fright of falling so fast in his flight, and admitted himself into the same hospital with his new illness. When the doctors saw he was a multimal they said, 'Please would you mind, kind find, if we snipped off one of your tails, as there's another multimal here who needs one bad.' Because remember—the one disadvantage every multimal has is he has to fly a hundred miles up into the sky once every year or die, and they said this other multimal had been in the hospital for almost that long. 'When another multimal comes in,' the doctors said, 'we'll have him give you one of his five tails. And that's what we'll do with each new multimal who checks in so none of you have to die.' Which in the end will mean they'll always be at least one multimal without a fifth tail. And in time, two to a few multimals flying around and maybe aground but if still able to get a hundred miles up in the sky, then only alive because of the bravery of brother multimals in surrendering one of their tails."

"If a multimal dies," Milly says, "and they get to him quick, they can cut off his tails and keep them in salt water and later use them to put on other multimals."

"There are no other multimals," Sharon says.

"But Paul said...the doctors said...the one in the hospital for almost a year? Then this story makes no sense."

"Because you're not listening right."

"So the Multimal said 'Sure, why not, docs? But I'd like snipping me tail off myself,' and he slipped his hoof under the sheet and gave the mop to the doctors. They thanked him and left. The Multimal said 'Chalk this day up as one of the most grueling in my life,' and fell asleep."

While waiting for the cake Sharon says "I love you, Paul, and don't want you to love another girl as much."

"Can't do. I've a little girl of my own and have to love her as much."

"You're a father? You never said. That's very sad for you. How old?" He opens his hand. "She must be very small and not as tall."

The cake's an opened storybook. Quixote, he supposes, judging by the upright candied characters. Its legend reads "For Sharon's 9th. Aren't you getting too old for inscribed birthday cakes? Either of you remember to buy candles? Love Mom and Dad."

"No and N O," Sharon says to the cake.

Shelly left a note and money. "Paul dear. We've no soda, ice cream, balloons, prizes, trumpery, paper napery, plastic silver. My last petition. Housekeeper's too busy preparing us for Fr. I'm shopping for noteworthy present for ours unruly. Half grinders minus onions and peppers at Gallucci's for 14 half sized guests and 1 ea unaltered for U, A & I. Loanx, S"

Later Paul writes Later Pete chaperoned Marta's party. The children played charades. "What am I?" Molly said, lying on her side on her arm, other arm flat on her free side, leg on leg, body stiff, eyes still, and when nobody guessed it, standing, nose chest toes touching the wall, legs joined, arms down her sides palms against thighs. "Then what now, dumbbells?" she said from the floor on her back, arms straight out palms outstretched, each spoken clue given between her hands flapping above her head and slapping the floor again. "Look is to see...Took is after you take... Cook is to make food and the person who makes it... Hook is to catch and the noun's the thing you catch it with...Rook is to steal...Crook is the stealer...Gook is sticky stuff...Fook could be a dirty word...Yook could be another way of saying you don't like gook or something hooked uncooked...Nook isn't a bird... Wook isn't a word..."

"No fair," Marta said. "Because no using even a single word."

"Tell us a spooky tale," Molly said. "Pete knows lots."

"I know that four tails do not a multimal aviator make."

"That tale's gibberish or a riddle," a boy said.

"If it's a riddle," Molly said, "then only Marta and I know the answer to it."

"I still think he's ding a ling bing," the boy said.

"You mean juts a tuts nuts," a girl said.

"Gad the mad dad," someone else said.

"Stop it moppet poppets Pete pleads."

"Then tell us the answer to the riddle."

"The answer to the riddle is a limerick. There once was a mick named Pick. Whose shtick was concocting a limerick. Till one day he whines. I loathe these five anapestic lines. Henceforth I'll only say A A B B A to make my limericks quick."

"You mean the answer to a limerick's a riddle," Molly said.

Sylvia appeared with a gift of gold earrings and an ear piercer. The ear piercer measured Marta's lobes, made her sit and sip cassis, said "I write about rites and yours is the mythic-traditional religio-societal one where the girl becomes the young woman for this is your initial penetration," and mumbo-jumboing after casting coins, bore the needle through Marta's lobe.

"You should've seen Mr. Shiliberti during the riting," the housekeeper said. "Two pillows stuffed to his ears and face deep in the bed."

"Holly, Molly and Arty," Pete said. "Came to Marta's party. The watches struck two. The needle stuck through. Oh my oh me oh Marta. Tell me why the woe of her foter. She's really not dead. It's all in his head. Could it be the dread of losing his baby doter?"

In the kitchen before supper that evening Shelly says, "Did you tell Sharon you spoke to your daughter last night?"

"I've made a couple calls I'll reimburse you for."

"The subject is why you said anything at all. She knows you were never married and associates children with marriage as much as I do and up to now didn't know what a real bastard was. I wish you'd occasionally behave as staidly as most of the harrowed characters in your stories and not always feel put on to blurt out your afflated secrets to the first easy believer who happens along. And what makes you so sure Lucia's yours?"

"Our blood group's the same. And ear lobes are supposedly inherited from the father and hers are like mine—big."

"Yours aren't big."

"She looks like me."

"Does she also hang like you?"

"I've photos. Several resembling snaps of me at her age when my hair was longer and lighter and face podgy and planed. Besides, she's already a greedy escapist reader and library browser and contrives and even tries to scribe stories in block print of girls like herself who write stories of girls like herself and her bonny mommy and dog called Miaow."

"If you're saying her heredity's single-sourced, Paul, it's monstrous."

"I don't like this galley scene."

"You'll like the denouement less if Rose suddenly divulges with pudding proof that she only said Lucia was yours to keep you sentimentally attentive and donatively warm. Or some baroque joke impostured by the proper poppa and herself to see how long you'd keep nibbling, biting and swallowing, yet still, torn lips and inadequate or foiled fill, swimming back and frolicking for more. But I've got to finish the *sole frite* and *saucisson.* Having fun? You seem to have goggly eyes and tizzied development for willowy Hil." Hilary, researcher for a newsweekly's Modern Living section and in a see-through T-shirt, sailed up from Manhattan today on a ketch of an atlasian nautical writer barely three times her age. She has a long ash on her cigarillo to get rid of and the man offers a cupped hand. Paul says to himself "From ashes to ashes."

"No," the man says, lip to lips with her, "with us it's soul to soul."

"What I mean was I thought Alain said your last name was Ashes. Just as I would have said, if you two were married, 'From Ashes' ashes to Ashes and back again,' if you had returned the ashes to her."

"You tell a wishy-washy line."

"Now Paul," Shelly says over salads, "can't stand any female writers."

"Not true. I can stand you."

"Only for personal reasons."

"Oh, yes?" Alain feigning concern.

"Because I'm Sharon's mama, by way of Sharon, Milly's friend-in-law, your old lady, now Hilary's buddy, though mostly because I'm his one host who hands him his own desk and thesaurus when he debuses and encourages him to work. But name one other lady writer you like."

"Joyce Cary? Evelyn Waugh?"

"Now you know you've told me their reputations far exceed their fulfillment and goals."

"She remembers everything I put down but nothing I say."

"Sharon wants to join us," Alain says, "but I told her it's too late."

"It's her birthday," Paul says. "How can she stay upstairs when her guests are clinking and shrinking to her good health and many mores?"

Sharon's sitting on the floor beside a phonograph, pasting today's birthday and last week's get-well cards into her scrapbook. A record of the First Family of the Moon is on. "It'll be through soon," she says. "Then you can carry me down."

"Despite the flights of unmanned reconnaissance spacecraft and manned landings on the moon," the record narrator says, "there are still unexplored and perhaps never-to-be-explored regions on the Earth's only natural satellite that are wholly composed of the cheese Carole the Cow's husband Carl makes from her milk. Their only child is called Chris. Now one day Chris wandered off too far from their secluded land of cheese and met a modern American Magellan named Aaron the Aerodynamic Geochronologist Astrophysicist. 'Who goes there,' Aaron said, 'friend or staff?' 'Why only a calf,'

Chris said, 'and you look so caricatural in your tubey puffed-up skin that I've got to laugh.' 'This skin is my astronautical suit and I'll be single props to hundred-thousand-pound thrusts that you lie,' and he packed Chris up in extra heavyduty polyethylene wrap and zapped him back to Earth as the first captured lunar spy."

The stories he gave Shelly to read are atop and atween her own manuscripts. Reading one he finished a few months ago, he's interested in learning how it ends. This one, written from March to June, is about his last love affair which lasted from December to March. In the story the woman said to Philemon "I haven't been sick the past week as I've been telling you till now on the phone, but fell in love with and now have living with me an Englishman." She said that "Since the day it started, I haven't had the guts to tell you this even one time." In the story every two sentences or mid and end of the same sentence rhyme. In real life he was living with her and after they were introduced to an Italian at a party, she said the man was greasy, overbearing, conceited, how she hates men so full of games to charm women and make them feel uptight. On the way home later on she told Paul she was in love with this man, he with her, they don't know how it happened or in what room it began, but in the kitchen they kissed, in the bathroom they took a bath, in a closet they conspired to meet for breakfast next morning which will ineluctably end up in bed in her bedroom in the afternoon, which is why she has to insist now that Paul move back with his folks tonight.

"Deciding flying wasn't for him," Paul says, "no matter how many mops he tied to his thigh—"

"You said his ass," Sharon says. "You're not a good reciter of children's stories, but I bet the Multimal is."

"He's more writer than reciter. And to write them he has this extra-large typewriter with keys the size and softness of blackboard erasers so he can slave away on them with his hoofs. One story I remember he wrote was about a man whose looks and past were quite like my own. But who acted nothing like me, as he kept making these faux-pas-la-ti-doe's like telling tales to girls who older adults thought were too young to hear. Or skedaddling from all the kids he'd helped make or got to know close and their mothers he'd boarded with, for he felt he was a bum dad and worse friend and was afraid of influencing these lovey coveys with the hectic hermitic life he led and ofttimes gloomy and giddy words he said that could cleverly or verily be misunderstood. And 'cause he knew he'd ne'er have the loot to suit these imps and moms and that by his nonpresence they might meet men who'd give them bon presents and huggier clothes and snuggier holes and send them to funnier schools and unchlorinated pools and where there'd be no lack and he'd heft them piggyback and be much sweeter and less fleetinger to them and their mammies, which'd make for merrier families. So P, the Multimal's l'homme who looked like me, ran, ran and ran away again and again and encore and why not once more? Till one day when he was thumbing on the road, a car stopped on a dime. P, quite broke, said, 'That's my dime your car stopped on,' and saw the driver was unlike any he'd seen. Five legs, six legs, seven necks, one baby tooth, half an ear, quarter for an eye, nickel for a nose, fifty-cent piece for a nare, thousands of dollar bills for hair, wallet for a mouth, checkbook for a tongue, debentures for decayed teeth, eeek, floating capital for saliva and bonds for gums, and this feast of a beast said, 'Hop in, me ami. Though car's too stingy for both you and your two bags and I. So cash in your typewriter and valise, deposit your clothes in your typewriter case and let's rip off and strike it rich and give credit only when it's overdue, son.' P did what he said. Scrapheaped his word machine and rucksack, squeezed in beside the Sundrymoneymal, wrote off his past at last and began a freer, sounder and more secure life."

The movie on his studio television set is about a young writer who trains to New York from the Old West with a huge novel and falls in love with a rich lady who acts and speaks something like Shelly. His editor is secretively in love with him and warns him about this older woman and her circle of culture hounds. "They have the single gift and unsparing craving of preying on talented writers and transforming them into unskillful puny hacks in half the time it takes me to edit their hulking novels in two. Leastwise with me the author has every right to reject my deletions and corrections, which if stubbornly done to excess could mean the manuscript's ultimate rejection no matter how fat the advance. While none of her young men have had the grit to resist being regaled and eventually devoured for new meat by the insatiable Hazel Brawn and her highborn ravenous friends."

"Since I suffer from the lifelong incurable disease of *cacoethes scribendi*, the writer says, 'they'll find me stuck in their throats or causing writer's cramps or blocks, but massively incapacitating."

"I still think you'll be what they eat."

One of the commercials ends with Anne Hathaway saying to Shakespeare, who's slavering over the cardigan sweater she bought him after he fretted about being frozen at his desk and unable to finish *Richard the Third*, "Well, as someone once said, Bill, 'All's wool that wraps Will.' Or was it 'Ill's Will no longer with his garret chill?' Or rather 'All's better in belles letters with a swell Metra sweater.'"

"You mean," Shakespeare says, "'All's ill that rends Will.'"

"Aye," Anne says.

"'Neigh' I should have the beleaguered Richard say."

During the movie Paul writes Lucia a letter. He folds the writing paper into quarters and with magic markers draws a picture in each square. The top right picture is of his face, the caption beneath reading "Hello, Lucia, I'm Paul, the man you telephone-talked to the other night, remember? I decided to send you this letter instead of a postcard—think back. As you can tell from that, I don't like repeating words like <u>remember</u> twice in so short a time made shorter by the necessary small writing, and I'm sorry not only for this long sentence which could have been broken up with a period in place of a comma 22 words and a contraction ago, but for using plurisyllabic words like <u>contraction</u>, <u>comma</u>, <u>period</u>, <u>sentence</u>, <u>necessary</u>, <u>repeating</u>, <u>decided</u>, <u>telephone</u> and maybe even <u>broken</u>, <u>only</u>, <u>sorry</u>, <u>writing</u>, <u>shorter</u>, <u>remember</u>, <u>postcard</u>, <u>letter</u>, <u>using</u> and maybe even <u>maybe</u> and even <u>even</u> and certainly <u>certainly</u> and <u>plurisyllabic</u>. I'm sure I left out one or two but not <u>one</u> or <u>two</u> since they're not plurisyllabic words. Though if I hadn't used all those underlined words in that sentence before last (please turn over and continue reading in box 1), the sentence would have read 'As you can see I don't like twice in so short a space made by the small, and I'm not for this long which could have been up with a in place of a but for words like and and.' Not that I've anything against that quoted sentence or couldn't find any meaning in it no matter how unwittingly it was written, I would have used *an* instead of <u>a</u> in

63

front of <u>in place of</u>. Anyway, I promise not to write
any more big words like <u>anyway</u> and <u>promise</u>. But
since I don't know whether you can read these big
words I promised I wouldn't write, I'll just write them
without assuming you don't know or can't read them
or that they can't be easily taught or explained to you.
Incidentally, I don't have yellow hair but felt I should
put that color in my first drawing since I already drew
my face red and neck blue.

"The above drawing in square B is my
dictionary. I don't think you'll be interested in seeing
it, but a book is a fairly easy thing to draw."

"Above is my typewriter. I write stories and
letters on it. This letter to you though I'm writing by
hand. I could write it by foot, but I have my slippers
on. The man in the first joke tells bad squares. Turn
that sentence around a snip and you'll see what I
mean when I say 'Maybe that's what makes his red so
face.' Turn 'red so face' around and you won't have a
proteron hysteron. Keep turning and you'll be dizzy.
(From now on TPO means <u>turn page over</u> so TPO
to box 2.) Getting back to the more woefully rollicky
topic of sad jokes and bad oxymora, I guess in my
second letter my face will have to be purple, which
might be your primary art lesson, if your mother
clears it up for you, though I won't tell you what I
heard or said to make my face that way.

"This is the room I'm currently visiting with
me lying on the floor in front of a turned-on television
set. The figure on the screen's left is a woman. One on
the right a man. Now the man's on the right and she's
on the left. Now she's cringing behind him. Now he's
cringing on top of her. Now a blanket's on top of them
both. Now a cat jumps on the blanket and snuggles in
between them. Now the light slowly goes off. (TPO
to box 3) Obviously I can't draw all these movements

and different light states in the little space I have for
the television screen in my drawing, so I'll leave the
figures the way I first drew them: two vertical lines
beside one another, the ganglier one standing for the
man, the small tire between them her television set,
the empty space in the tire the animated TV screen.
By the way, what I seem to be poking with a big stick
in this drawing is the letter I'm writing to you now.
And still now. And until I stop writing this letter. One
day I hope to see you where you live or where I live
which as I told you on the phone is several hours away
from you in New York by plane. That's bad English
(please continue on page 2), but the only language I
know well enough to illiterately know. The man in
squares A and D on page 1 makes veriberi bad jokes,
or tries to, as he just tried to, and unfailingly fails,
as he just succeeded in unfailingly failing again, and
again. What is the color of dumbness? Which is the
color I'd draw the man's face in those two pictures if
I hadn't already drawn them read I mean red? That's
even worser English, and what I just wrote then the
worsest, and there can't be any worse English more
than that, except maybe that, if I hadn't capitalized the
E in *anguish* and made it *i*.

 "P.S. The movie I'm watching ends with this
rich lady getting sick from a strange disease known
as kakemonomania scribbadibblerbe, and the fiction
writer in the film, ten years younger than me and
whose name I think is Pom, saying, as she lies asleep
in her hospital suite bed, 'I've had enough of you and
your lowdown friends for a lifetime, Mrs. Brawn,
and I only wish I had the pluck and spunk to say it
to your face,' which he actually is since she's lying
on her back. The young lady editor, which to make a
long story short is a worker who makes tiny sentences
and spaces out of toiled-over compressed passages and

venturesome paragraphs, loves Pom or Rom or some hom-nom like Dom or Strom but only one of thom, comes to the hospital room and she and the writer hug and mug. The unedited editor says 'You were really in love with her, weren't you, and there's nothing in life worth living for more than that, in spite of it so frequently ending in agony, fiasco and utter distress,' and he nods yes-es-es. 'Will you two idiots please get the H out of here,' the older woman says. 'I'm bushed with you both and want to get some shuteye,' and they smile at her, she at them, they leave the room, race down the stairs and through the lobby and in front of the hospital he hails a cab, they run to it hand in hand while the doorman yells after them 'Well that sure must have been a quick recovery,' for you see, Lucia (as the closing credits come on and the cooing muzak whoops it up and their cab pulls away with the couple visible through the rear window kissing to beat the band), when the two of them came to the hospital separately a few minutes ago (TPO), the doorman saw they were both very sad.

"No no, all wrong. Say, who do I think I'm writing this letter to anyway? Maybe to Anyway, but can you say all that? Not 'all that' but what I wrote before I wrote 'Maybe to Anyway, but can you say all that?' But I'm about as adept at sending off epistles to bissles as I am missles. I mean missives to magaths as I am apostles. But there, you see, Lucie? Too much effort. Too many wisecracks, lies, tricks and gimcracks. There again. Never ends. In edition t'ill wit y'll git whit I premised mit (please T to new P last time)," and he draws a fullscale facsimile of the message-address side of a straddle-backed Don Q attacking a tilted windmill, and on the left side above his meticulously printed "Made in Spain (reproduccion prohibida)," he writes "Dear Lucia:

Here's the picture postcard I said I'd mail all alone. Having fun. Hope you are too. Wish you were here. Wisch Ich war deux. That heroic grave structure on the card's front is not the posh posada I'm posing at but this country's largest bibliocrypt photographed right after its heaviest snowfall in 50 years. Kindest regards to your mom. Love, Paul."

He dials Oregon direct. "By way of telegrammic telegraphese and telltale telic exegeez, this tel-l-e-o-fanatico televiewing telluric teleman tells telephone that Tilly woman wife same short story Rose Lucia Lucia's fictitious sister in. Real life Tilly not wife and son same story real life non son too. Her phone stings. 'It's you,' Tilly'll say. 'I figured you'd call tonight.'"

"Oh it's you," Tilly says. "I figured you'd call tonight."

"Just as I figured you'd say 'Oh it's you, I figured you'd call tonight,' exce fo d oh."

"But you always call while I'm writing you a letter. This one's a month in the making, as I wanted to get it all down so I can put you out of my head for good. Do you realize we haven't seen you for three years? That was in the letter. But why'd you call? That of course was not. Assuaging your guilt again? A wee drunk or high or both or depressed or desperate to hear our cheering voices again or none or some of those or all or more?"

"Why didn't you send Ezra to me for the summer as I asked you to? Or at least write you weren't going to or why you couldn't?"

"If you're ready I'll tell you what I think of your relationship with Ezra and save myself the chore and cost of completing and posting this letter. Naturally I intend to be brutally frank. Not that I imagine anything I say could do more than injure you for a few seconds—your ego, but you've got that coming too."

"Ready as EverReady was, Frank."

"You're a fool, Paul. Your copout is harder to understand than Ezra's real father and more unforgiving in my mind. You had his love and trust. He used to tell people 'I have two dads. Wolf Bowers is one, but my real dad is Paulie.' You earned that distinction, exactly as I earned the love Ezra gives me. Parents deserve whatever feelings they get from their children, whether love or hate. My parents earned my mistrust. You walked away, turned your back on Ezra and said, 'You don't count, kid. What I'm doing is more important than you. I'm gonna stay in New York and become somebody. I'm gonna write fantasies and someday some wise important writing man will come along and say "Hey, Paul Clay, you're somebody." And Ezra, old colt, that's winning. Then I'll be a star.' Swell. Only it may happen when you're 60 years old—lonely, bitter and broken. How can you continue to expose yourself to the useless asslicking overpraise you get or the steady stream of rejection slips from pedants of a system you know is false? If it's so important to be published or read, why don't you tack up your prose on public walls like one of those gas parades or last narrades or what did you say the name of those French scrolls on fences were, or just look elsewhere—a small private firm? The Russet Bus Crazies picked up a hitchhiker who had a book about Vietnam that none of the major publishing houses would touch because it didn't jive with their ofay corporate state straights. So Eugene Smiley, the dude with all the bread, said he'd publish it for him. That was two months ago and it's ready to go to press."

"That's very swift."

"I said it took two months. I've read a copy in manuscript and it's a super book. Naturally, you wouldn't like it. But you didn't like the *Last Job Globe Datagrog Sequel* that Herb put out, while I enjoyed reading his stuff and everybody else's in it too. I wish you'd stop panning things that aren't produced by so-called serious artists. The *Sequel* was definitely a family affair—a family making money and having a ball. West Coast humor really offends the polished East Coast sense of propriety. Poor Paul. You're really a product of the New York Jewish syndrome. I was just remembering all the people and projects you were always picking apart. So smug and cocksure you were, never thinking that some of your own crit might apply to you."

"What?"

"Crit. Crit. That it works both ways. Am I a thorn in your side, Paul?—platitudinous as that must sound to you. I recall so many a long and lofty address by you concerning man's inhumanity to man. But I'd like to know what you've done in your 35 years besides take care of an invalid father and a slice of the burden off your sorrow-sick mother, though even there I bet your reasons are guilt or something unhealthy. You make me angry. You're a thorn in my side too. I think you're blowing it, my man. An oversimplified flash I just had is that you've repudiated a life force in influence—meaning Ezra and Lucia—and accepted a non-life force in your parents, rejection slips, words rather than action, love stories rather than love, sycophantic mealymouths, agents who can't sell, editors who can't get you published, publishers who wish you'd wise up and go away, New York. Substitute positive for negative if you want—it's all the same. I've been seeing too many Bergman and Rohmer flicks. I let two or three pass this week cuz they're so heavy. But there you have some of my impressions concerning you and Ez. It's all in my letter which I guess I can rip up now. But how do you feel about my speech? Was I very hard on you for a change?"

"Mail it if you'd like. I could switch it around as you say and use it as a job résumé. And nowanights I am usually ready for wear. Though a lot of what you said I can with a heart of holes subscribe to and which is why I wanted to begin making it up to Ezra by having him here this summer and longer if he liked."

"He didn't want to go. He told me he told you on the phone he did because he didn't want to hurt Paulie's feelings. He doesn't want to be alone with you. He's scared you might suddenly split on him again and then he'd be stranded in that smelly insane city. And why would a boy want to stay with your sick parents?"

"I thought it'd be educative. He'd see how we take care of my dad. My mother would have been very sweet to him. My father hardly speaks and except for exercise and meals usually sleeps, so most of the time he wouldn't have known Ezra was around. And for six weeks we had this dreamy beach cottage on a dramatic stretch of shoreline on the Sound."

"You want to see him that much, come out. They've planes whizzing to Oregon. You'd have to flop out with one of our friends, as we're short of space here. And Sher would get so threatened with you crashing on our scene that he'd up and leave us without notice and then Ezra would drub your nuts for life."

"Is Ez in?"

"Can you afford this call, cuz I can call back. We've a magic tillyphone. Nobody we know fusses with phoning LD anymore on their own nums. But you'd probably think that dishonest."

"It isn't?"

"But deserting a boy when he loves you,
that's not. Ah, that's snot. You're sick. Not crazy
ga-ga or mad as a hatter's patter sick, but twisted,
misshapened—wicked prick sick. Paul, before you go
there's one thing I've just now made a decision on
after deliberating about it for weeks."

"Here comes execution."

"If you do turn up here, then we'll certainly see
you if you sack out at a hotel or on somebody else's
floor. But till then I don't want you calling or writing
Ezra again."

"Not even his birthday?"

"Not even his wedding. If we ever do layover
in your city, we'll ask your mother where you are, but
you probably shouldn't even come out before then."

"What about Christmas and Pesach and
Twelfth Night and Saint Pat's and Lincoln's and
Washington's and Father's and Forefathers' and All
Fool's Day?"

"It's what I want."

"But he takes for granted my hush money and
doles. And not only on his natal and noel, but there's
my traditional Easter-suit-and-shoes gift every May
Day and B.V.D.'s every V.E. and J."

"Truth is it's unhealthy your correspondence
and calls. Boys need men. So let Ezra forget you and
get to know his real father better or even Sher or some
other man or Big Brother if Sher slips away. I've
forgotten you."

"In piecemeal or block? Even those great
mate creative dinners we used to make where we got
slopped and never went by the book?"

"It took a while, I won't deny. But children
forget easier."

"And those mammoth emoluments I conferred upon you every Friday?"

"Two and three part-times a week you had running concurrently, and if I'd have hatched the child you sighed for so much, it still would have had to have been born on the street."

"I did your gardening well."

"You slew my immortal Sweet Williams and live-forevers and never could do away with those damnable bees."

"I wasn't a killer."

"Not even when they caused those elephantiasic bites on Ezra's lips and eyes?"

"I mowed your lawns."

"Not as well as ten-year-old Ariel across the street."

"She used her dad's electric."

"It at least cut the grass close. But you, you big dope, didn't want to pay her the every-other-week two bucks."

"Why should I when I was willing to cut it with the hand mower?"

"Because you'd bitch about mowing whenever I asked. And then in the end when you finally consented, the grass would have grown too high to cut with my mower, so I always had to call in Ariel no matter what. Isn't it all coming in loud and clear yet, Paul? There was nothing you could do but write. You'd hole up and funk-fill my guest room turned writer's sty every chance you got. If you had looked for a single normal-paying job and made writing your lesser pursuit for a while, we might still be living in California together instead of us in this Oregon dungeon and you in New York doing what you are. But you wouldn't. You said you couldn't. 'Goddamnit, I can't,' you said, 'so please please leave me be.' That was you. Screaming like a failed queer. Totally beyond hope. You couldn't even fix a sink washer, install my stereo, give a car a tuneup, even set up my beautiful brass bedstead that had to lie under the mattress gathering dust for three years till Sher came. You couldn't do anything useful except occasionally create original dinners and replace simple light switches and uncomplicated lamp plugs."

"I used to replace simple light switches and uncomplicated lamp plugs."

"Don't forget the original dinners."

"You used to hold me tight at night."

"I'd hold any man tight I'd let in my bed."

"You used to say I showed good taste and know-what when we went to auctions and antique shops."

"All those great goodies I let get by because we didn't have the bread have since risen 500 percent. But enough. And I insist. If you call and Ezra doesn't answer first, I'll hang up. And whatever mush you write and drawings you send him I'm going to collect one by one and once a year lump into a bundle and return them in one of the hundred manila envelopes you left behind. As for me, there can't be any but the most morbid reasons why you'd ever want to contact me again."

"I could want to find out how your folks are."

"See ya, Paul."

"And the weather. If I were ever planning on journeying to Ashland I might want to know if the sun or rain's out and what kind of clothes and shoewear I should wear."

"I'm getting him for you for the last time, Paul. E.Z.?"

"What if I wanted to call to tell you about my folks? Or how the weather is in New York and what shoewear you should wear?"

"Hello?"

"Hi, wiseguy, how's tricks?"

"No tricks now, jokes. Want to hear one that's
funny?"

"Bombs away."

"A lady gets on a plane with her son named
Heinie."

"And midflight Heinie gets swooshed out
the emergency door and the lady says to the pilot—
whoops, mussed up your joke again."

"Did you do," Tilly says. "But he's got more.
Reads those crummy jokebooks all day."

"Do not."

"Does nothing else. Blew a month's wad on
them this week. Takes them to the crapper, bed, and in
class Mr. Sunshine said—"

"Maaa, will you get off the phone?"

"*Maaa*, is that what Mr. Sunshine said?"

"He'll chew your ears off with those duds, Paul.
Don't let him tell you more than ten. See ya, stooge."

"I know another good one," Ezra says.

"Hellooo?" Shelly says from downstairs.

"Goshdarnit, Ez, someone just came in. I'm'n'a
have to bust this up now and try to call you back."

"Why, where are you?"

"Away. And cripes, now a whole crew of
stewed flu-ridden freaks are barging in, trashing up
my floor, tramping on my anemones. One of em's
even coming at me with a rope, got me with it by the
throat, and now he's trying to take the phone. Hey—
aagh—cut it out, not the phone but your hand, *arretez,
tenez!* I couldn't even hear you if we spoke. I love you.
You're the best little boy in the whole white world.
But I've got to go."

"I'm not little. I used to be, when I said that for

wide world, but now I'm bigger."

"I know. I forgot. What a lapse. But say you love me a little also, Ez."

"I love you a little also, Ez."

"My crimes. Is nothing sacrosanct? Tief, tomb burglar, line lifter, Captain Kidd. I'll call back tonight, I swears. Phone signal between us will be—if it zings once, then stops, then zings a minute after, then in plain English grab it, got me?"

"You really can't hear my joke?"

"Didn't you in that love-you-a-little-also poke just tell it?"

"That was no joke."

"What you say, young man? Ca harly hear ya. Weak chouder. Prittle powwowfuler."

"Yes or no?"

"Pardon me, Paul," Shelly says. "I didn't know you were on the phone."

"Shoot."

"A man—I mean a boy gets on is in a classroom and says to his teacher 'I've got to go to the bathroom.' The teacher says 'Not before you do your ABC's.' So the boy starts 'ABCDEFGHIJKLMNOQRST...'"

"You forgot the P."

"That's the joke."

"How can that be the joke?"

"Because the teacher says after the boy said RST 'What happened to the P?' And the boy says 'It's running down my leg.' Isn't that a good one?"

"Never alpha better coprophiliac. Listen for my broken rings, champ."

"When? Later?"

"Why do you write?" Shelly says.

"Because there's air?"

"No, seriously."

"No seriously because they're ears? Eras ere?

T'err is Eire? Yare fare more? *Mere* fore bore? There
are theres and ares and yores and lores and therefores?
I can't ans. Got rants in my pants. Why do you
write?"

"It's a very foolish question. As a writer I'd
never ask it of myself or of another writer and I
wouldn't expect another writer to ask it of me. But
why do you write?"

"Because snare's snuffing snew sunder sur
snun."

"What's snew?"

"Why indite recourse writs the none procession
pat feast whores me, host indoses and sexbites me,
and woe data now touch I light relieve shat bare his
puffing do cite, sat I savant the sour and lability phoo
fight, fat wry probingly won't Steven tike do like, sly
will delight reclause I reel goblurged screw exspritz
mysulf, tow I ill row reverysing I sit just fend win
dinspritzable wailure."

"Slop."

"Writing gives me the greatest opportunity
available to be the biggest failure imaginable."

"Shop."

"No, everything I've said so far's been said in
more sibilant surds sand saw sore sensible seasons sigh
suther switers seesaw see."

"Stom."

"Or else all I've said so far has come from what
I've heard or read or may not even be the original
thoughts and sayings of the persons I heard or read or
heard read or heard they'd read, written or said and
in fact I might have completely misunderstood these
thoughts and sayings, so what I think I'm repeating
here shouldn't be ascribed to anyone but me."

"Atop."

"I don't know why I write. I do think I'll

continue to write. I'll continue to write because I must write. I must write because I must express myself. I must express myself because it's the only way to continue. I must continue because I find it's the only way I can write. I must write because I find it's the only way to continue to write and to continue to continue and to continue to express myself and to find. I must find because I find it's the only way to continue to find."

"Stob."

"Pits were homey bay wive forsaking a misgiving. Ride he mutterly juiceless mewing manyling ouch. Guy lust do rain fatmention and dafiction above mothers."

"Swop."

"I want to give pleasure to people."

"Scop."

"Wruting jesterfies me."

"Stot."

"Bye cunt whew ache splicitimy bout of simplicity, cimploxety rout of complexity."

"Sleep, Paul."

"No. Writing redeals thongs stout by stealth mat far alonely resealed shrew my writing. I smite he snores high Sam clever yo rappy mas ten mime writing. Writing, I refeat's, she moanly say I show now you take a giving."

"That you, Paul?" Tilly says.

"I told Ezra I'd call back."

"Was that you with the single ring just before?"

"It's part of a phone summoning system Ezra and I devised. The first one's to warn him not to answer the next call when it's anticipated you'll hang up on me. The third call, coming seconds after the second, is the tipoff for Ezra to charge across the street watchful of cars, dogs, logs, fogs and polliwogs to

Helen Elsmen's house to get my call all agog there, as from the third call on it's expected you'll demand the phone be kept off the hook."

"Not after the third call but now."

"Rats lot hollowing me stript, Nilly."

Paul's awakened and watches from the street a morning parade composed of a brass band playing a ceaseless Portuguese dirge, Scouts and Brownies of two states shaped into a marching CONNERI, priest and mayor sitting side by side in a convertible bearing the Dodge dealer's compliments on aprons on the car's doors, volunteer fire brigade engines with their sirens humming and police chief's car with its roof light teetotuming, women's auxiliary corps rolling and unraveling bandages as they walk, fishermen reweaving a single seine on top of a trailered fishing boat, National Guard ambulances, Civil Defense Jeep, state trooper black maria, bookmobile, veterans of several foreign wars, limousine of Gold Star mothers, mitted Little and Pony Leaguers tossing up hardballs, two battle-dressed and -painted descendants of the area's 17th-century Indians on unicycles, Forest Service bulldozer, town warden's tree-trimming truck, village street sweeper and scrubbed-down private sanitation van, floats with five-foot-high letters of blue flowers against a green floral background saying LABOR DAY AD 71, girl, followed by a column of girls in similar white floor-length gowns and veils, carrying on a cushion the regional cathedral's Virgin statue crown, bus that will drive the brass band and crown to parades today in other towns.

In the studio Paul writes the first draft of a story about a bookbinder who makes a series of phonecalls to the same woman. She says in the first lines that she's sorry but she's going to be too busy studying all day and night: he'd invited her to a museum member's preview of an exhibition of incunabula and illuminated lettrines. He phones her repeatedly to accompany him and she gets more and more upset she might not pass tomorrow's civil service bibliotherapist test and begins to realize how disturbed the man she thought she was falling for actually is. His last call to her at 4 a.m. is answered by a librarian on her apartment building floor who she's asked to stay the night with her in case the phoning bookbinder tries breaking down her door. The story ends with the narrator, now nicknamed Pill by the woman, talking to them as they on this first day they really meet lie asleep in bed, saying she knows he doesn't like speaking like this, with no one speaking back, that he must sound vertiginously verbigerative to her, to them, like the insane Danish monologist about to sprout his dudgeon through the drapes, though all he wants is for her to say she's listening if need be with her librarian listening, just as he's now crying uncle, huing e's carbuncled though still gruntled, but an end, again, to his lexiphanic longiloquent antidisestablishmentarianisming, since he wishes to whisp crisp and lisplessly that he's never phoned anyone more than three to four times in a day before and by her leisure now he vows not to allow this routine to happen again, he slights his froth, he sweers, but she must see he felt and still feels compelled, all right deranged, admittedly she must be repelled his acting so untypically strange, but he clearly got caught up in the rut of making these calls, sorely she can understand, certainly her librarian samaritan must have come across quick-lived anankastic cases such as his in the billion books and poems and tomes he's scanned, aiee, i.e., though why doesn't she hang up on him, or hang up and then uncradle the receiver on him, or maybe she likes him babbling on babily like this, it can't be as she said she can stand the continuous telephone company whine that her phone's off the hook less, help him, save him, no, he'll be okay, fugacious obtestation, -trunctation and –umbration, in five years and a day, or in the time it takes to drop by her place, which he'll be doing just as soon as he gets off the phone, not as soon as he gets off but in the time it takes to get to her place right after he pianorollissimoly hangs up on her here at his home, speak, he pleads, "Please speak," are his last words, "Phil's importuning you to at least pease peep, my sad Jane Madelaine."

Shelly calls. "Country club for conch?"

"Mrs. her room," housekeeper says.

"*Paulie.*"

"Sharon woning down the rinding stairs, bidding her bitsy body be boisted and bugged."

"I love you so much," Sharon says. "Adieu."

"I do."

"Meantime, find something to read," Shelly says to him. "And these?" packing his manuscripts. "Can I take them on the *France*? I'll be tied up till then and you've extra copies, *n'est-ce-pas*?"

"Nest snuff."

Alain overheard in the adjoining room "Corot, 24 x 36 in, oil, although not prized landscape, realistic or poeticized, is popular woman-interrupted-reading genre. Woman, head to toes, nude, twentysoish young, three-quarters buttocks and back, one quarter front, breasts exposed, plump, nothing more lowly or provokingly shown, meaning woman predominantly though not superabundantly plump, escalading staves of tub, overabundantly I mean, take it from breasts exposed, breasts and nipples exposed, full breasts and erect nipples exposed, woman not redundantly plump, stepping into tub, one foot as if testing

temperature with toes, other foot raised in preparation
to placing both feet in and body to bathe, burnished
hair long, combed, book in hand outthrust behind
her above inlaid floor, fingers established between
pages as bookmark, robe, towel, smaller book and
soap in soap dish on stool. Met and Chic Art Inst
have several paintings of same category—eliminate
'erect'— all interrupted readers, grandly or amply
dressed. One Met oil with identical model, perhaps
wife or demimondaine or main animating spirit,
called 'Interrupted Reading,' clothed and bonneted on
garden bench, no toilette. No no toilette. Our present
minimum price, future value incomputable—"

    While Shelly packs, Paul reads the second-to-
last story he completed, the one an editor said will end
his collection she'd like published if her house accepts
it. "This story should give the reader an especially
good end-of-book feeling," she wrote, "after so much
escaping, absconding, uprooting, defecting, despair."
Of it a magazine fiction editor wrote "Isn't this 'soap
opera' piece n-fiction, and if it is, shouldn't you like to
send it to our articles editor instead?" His agent said
"Maybe I'm missing some of it, but what is Patrick,
a deaf mute?" The story's about an operator of a one-
man ultramodern nonpolluting shredding machine
of a publishing company's unremaindered books,
who fantasizes having a relationship with a woman
he sees on the street every weekday morning as they
head to work. Last spring Paul was subbing at a public
intermediate school near his home and saw a young
woman on the street every weekday morning except
holidays who he thought attractive and intelligent-
looking but never had the courage to approach. Patrick
accidentally knocks a jar of instant tea out of her
supermarket cart, suggests he acquit himself over
real or iced tea with her after he cleans up the mess,

asks her out for dinner, dates her, mates her, they become engaged, married, prospective parents, all as he previously fantasized with her, she persuades him to undermine and then gasoline bomb what she calls his concentrated extermination camp and to make peace with his conscience and the bones and drones of live and dead authors everywhere by opening a used bookshop with a small printing press. Paul watched her write her name and address on a supermarket delivery sticker, some days walked out of his way to pass her brownstone and look at what could be her 5A front windows, checked the telephone directory for her phone number and noted it in his address book though knew he had no intention of ever calling her, once followed her to the subway, stood in the same crowded car, got off to change trains and bought the same newspaper and turned to the book review page as she immediately did, in the abutting car took the express downtown, tailed her along rush-hour streets till she entered a bookstore, from the sidewalk saw her minutes later with a salesperson's tag on the store's dickey collar and a salesbook clasped to her belt, sort, uncrate and stack records and books till the store's doors opened, punched in at school more than an hour late and around eight dollars was subsequently deducted from his monthly paycheck.

Now, he would like to, in this day and age, right here, on this very spot, today, not tomorrow, this time at present, from these moments right now till he says stop, oh don't be ridiculous, come off it, who would have thought it? let the gentleman speak, I'm truly amazed, he's saying he'd like to, what are you talking about? where do you get that stuff? will wonders never cease? I declare, does he ever, I'm truly amazed, poppycock, beans, baloney, you slay me, horse manure, where does it all come from? be with a

woman like that woman in that story he wrote who
was, act your age, grow up, don't make me laugh, how
you do come on, big joke, stop kidding yourself, breaks
me up, laugh a minute, or as he thought that young
woman he saw on the street every working weekday
morning was, oh yeah, go on, pull my other sleeve,
no thank you, oh you kid, that's what you say, maybe
I'm wrong, in a pig's eye, bless my heart, it's got bells
on it, what a crack, a crock, soft, warm, loving, sweet,
sensible, strong and kind, come come, now I'll tell
you one, like fun, well I'm a monkey's uncle, do you
feature that, better you than me baby, tell it to the
Marines, it beats the Dutch, funny as a rubber crutch,
get off my foot, ouch you're killing me, as I live and
breathe, I'm truly amazed, not to be believed, pshaw,
sheet, shucks, I'm from Missouri, you don't say? it's
true, says you, I'll be jiggered, what a nerve, shut my
mouth, clap my trap, shiver my timbers, blow me
down, strike me dead, for crying out loud, what now?
dog my cats, tickle my willies, goodness, gracious, my
stars, heavens and earth, dear me, for Pete's sake, what
do you know, twaddle, indeed, zounds, fiddledeedee,
adzooks, gad so, good luck, the devil you say, t'aint
so McGee, pile it on, blimey, bushwah, hogwash,
hooey, hoopdedoodle, nibbledenoodle, my word,
what now? run off at the mouth, bilge, bosh, bah,
balderdash, pishpash, pashpish, what piss, rubbish,
raspberries, horsefeathers, hominy grits, sticks in your
throat, in your hat, don't give me that, bullcrap, far
be it from me, I see, oh brother, let's hear another,
hind, wind, strung, tweet, tensible, hoving, soft, sift,
saft, shift, insensible, reprehensible, finndensunable,
ope sopperer, mope slopperer, nope whopperer, op
cropperer, plop, flop, clop clop, now now, there there,
warm warm, simmer simmer, down down, cool off, go
slow, steady as she blows, easy there mate, take a rest,

time for recess, calm yourself, come to your senses, smarten up, get hep, be wise, mind out, relax, have a seat, load off your feet, watch your step, look sharp, here comes cookie, you'll be okay, thataway, I believe you, sure we do, what rot, enough of that.

"Grief, Paul," Shelly says. "Your own story stabbing you so? Hold on for two secs."

Not someone like the woman in his story with that Italian or was he an Englishman? Certainly someone like the woman in his story who nursed him and then bused them through barrier blocks from one to another enslaved land. Not someone like the woman aloft on the trapeze bar who licked his lips, lids and forehead as she let his wrists go. Maybe someone like the woman who stayed unperturbably beside him in their flat in the apartment building the revolution- or reactionaries were about to blow. Nor someone like the woman he and their son stalked to make sure the rock musicians she favored didn't beat on her face. In the story Terry said "Do you mind if I go, Po?" and all he had to do was say no and she wouldn't as she wanted to stay while he preferred her away and he didn't care where or with whom as long as she averted getting hurt and returned before he left for work so he said "If that's what you want, have fun, one on me, whatever that might be, double entente, troupe disentendering" nigh about the turn in their tie when he was proroguing his own going with Tilly owing to Ez. He should call Ez now to explain some things. Ez, I've got to squeak past for x-reasons I plant cain. Better a letter dispatched to Helen Elsmen's with a note attached saying "Pleez geev this to Ease as a surpreez." Ez wants a sprise. Got a purise for I's, Pie? Lap, sid to read. Up, god be raised. Arms, snoogle and cud. Now Ez turn to read. Words downslide up. I know that picture means. High, farrer than the sky. Down, em tie or uv gah to may. Wraaah, doe waana go to beg. Swish off de lie, turn on dee on. I doe wan de bee in de dar alo, so key bo begroo door oen. I luf you, Police, whir all my haar. Hey you, Poor, you're so bear en me t'me. Dearest Ezra, I still think of you as one of the wisest, slyest, hippest, flippest, slickest, wickedest, stingiest— Dear Ez, I feel you're old enough now to understand that the reasons I left so suddenly three years ago weren't as a result of anything you or Tilly did but— Back, give me piggypack. Glass, let's click-click. Wipe, my milk slight spilled lips. Run, I'm won. I'm faster. Going be strongaller. Dear sir, prior to our phone conversation on or before the evening of September 4th, 1971, I spoke with your mother, Mrs. Bowers, who during the same call, but in advance of our own dialogue, broached what I believe should be more thoroughly developed in our future written communication. Most Reverend Master, may I humbly beseech your undulgence for the callous indifference and ofttime deplorable inattention I've displayed in relation to— Your Grace, Reader of Ghosts, Liver of Kings, Nero's Pleasure Peeper, Detector of Gearls, what explanation could I afford to put forth, without the most diligent distortion of truth and ensuant likeliness of a good garroting, that could enucleate any further what you undoubtedly discerned through my absence and all but silence. Buddy, Chum, Crony, Confidant, Partner, Best Friend, Bosom Pal, greetings, psst, yo-ho, oh-le-ee-oh-lei-ee-yoo, howdy do, how de do, how d'ya do, are you? 's tricks? every little thing? world treating you? I'm fine, long time no see, funny gag your ABCP, miss ya, kiss ya, love ya, wanna see ya, what can I say? maybe one fine day, try and understand, so hard to explain, though know full well, realize straight out, be aware of to the very end, that O, ah me, woe betide,

poor dear, alas, lackadaisy, have mercy, what a pity, so
sorry, but do me a favor, just one thing I ask, bear in
mind that, regardless of whatever else happens, despite
anything anyone might tell you, needless to say,
remember too, take care, godspeed, look after yourself,
best of health, peace be with you, don't want to hear
any bad reports, be good, keep in touch, stiff upper
lip, compliments to your mom, kind remembrances
home, fond memories from afar, with all due respects,
excusing the liberty, in deference to, love, yours
affectionately, best wishes, most respectfully, I remain
friendly yours, sincerely, may God bless you, through
thick and thin, years on end, till hell freezes over,
cordially, always and forever and a week of Sundays
and month after month and year in year out, yours
truly till the cows come home again for a dog's age
faithfully, Paul, P, Pi, Po, Pum.

  While prizes are being presented on the
country club lawn for the best by sex and age division
in boating, swimming, diving, riding, tennis, skittles,
shuffleboard, sea shell and pine cone assemblages and
sportsmanship, a woman asks Paul "Are you picking
up any good material in our village?"

  "The material in the city is both superior in
quality and variety and less dear."

  "Nearly amusing, but surely, you must confess,
as I can't deny, there are some character types of
certain interest here, which as a writer, as we all are,
around this table that is, which isn't to say there aren't
only writers around other tables nearby, or elsewhere,
but someplace on the grounds I mean, where there are
tables of course, or anything resembling tables which
people can sit around like this, the bowed bar for
instance, the round raft in the water for example, my
they give out a lot of laurels and awards, must always
model his characters on real people and true emotions,

don't we all agree?"

"Everyone has his own system. Mine depends on what your measurements are, meaning glove, shoe, hat, sock and belt size, and whether you're small, medium, large or extra large, and is that expanded, regular or collapsed? Or maybe women's shirts don't run that way and they only take a stretch and slip off and it's the stockings I'm thinking of that pop off or slacks which if they're pressed too much tear away. Speaking about stepping on it, I'll have to be moseying off for New York now to set foot there by a fall night."

"Stay," Shelly says in the studio. "Only through tomorrow when you'll get the boxes to pack my bed."

"*Vite vite*," she says. "I still have to dress, undress, redress and dress again."

At the Bustelli cocktail party Paul asks a model exhibit builder for Manhattan's natural history museum whether he had anything to do with making its transparent lifesize female manikin that lectures on its lit-up anatomy parts and their functions.

"My boy, that was before my time. But listen to this gem. While doing repair work on what I've sibilously rechristened our stark Sadie of the sonics, I possibly became the first fully maturated male to get a hernia from picking up a plastic doll."

"You mean a hisnia," Alain says.

Paul drinks to that, to this, to the other thing, too much, to Shelly "Tonight I'll drink two less and ditch the dinner party to toddle off for some needful sleep."

"You must come. They'll have the best spread and most appealing people in tow."

Hilary's there. "Excuse me," she says just as he reaches her through the crowd, "but I was told I should meet an important editor who I see came in. I'm ready for a promotion or new position and he's also with the magazines."

"*The* magazines. The famous Magazines? Not the Famous Magazines, but just those likeable easygoing accomplished Magazines who are so well-balanced and dependable and have been around so long? And the Loves, Pulps, Dicks and Periodicals, are they here too? And what about the Chrestomathes and Selihoths and Garlands, Enchiridions, Screeds, Psalters and Apercus? And can you see the old Battledores and royal Kalendars and congressional records and petty Cashbooks and round Robins and Bill Boards and Pat Ristics and O.F. Fares, U. Kase, A.C. Rostic, T.E.L. Estich and Al Bum, Doc Ket, Pop Novel, Ma Nual, Pastor Al Epistle, Reb Us and Tex Tus and Lex Icon and Cy Clopedia and Hy Etograph, Abe Cedarium, Ono Masticon, Lo Gogogram, Flo Rilegia, Pan Dect, Kit Sch, Sale E. Scheck, Ann O. Tation and Miss Ive and Penny Dreadful?"

"You're blocking my passage?"

"Still pooped?" Shelly says.

A natural history writer who he's giving his views against group therapy for writers to says "Stop lecturing me. Why do you think you know so much? Where is your documentary proof? When were you in analysis? Who have you studied with? What monographs have you read? Then how can you be so patronizing and intractable? I won't listen to this, can't. Don't gadfly me. Buzz off. I'm already repelled by you. Without even knowing you. But I can tell by your vulpine eyes, leonine mien, piggish aims, peacockish clothes and high-flying tone."

A woman he's telling a true serious story to says "Do I descry a note of dissembling in your voice?"

"No, of admiration."

"Hilary," he says, "like to go for a walk?"

"Whatever for?"

"Because it's not about to come to us?"

"To me," he overhears, "non-nonfiction writers are incurable thumb-suckers who can only talk and write to one another or to themselves."

"Excluding our own Shelly and Marco of course."

"It's got to be tough for anyone to talk with his thumb in his mouth," Paul says, "and tougher yet to two-hand type that way."

"If you write fiction," the man says, "then I apologize not for what I said but for saying it too loud."

"Hilary," Paul says, "like a refill?"

"No, thanks, I'm still nursing my first."

"It's always so wholesome and quieting when a woman nurses in public."

"Listen Paul," someone says, "—Paul's it, right? Well, if anytime you want to communicate with someone, let me know."

"I thought I'd be rendering this village a service and kind of honor by writing about it," Marco says. "Now I find they want to write me off on my tail. I mean run me up without nails. I mean off me right—"

"You brought it notoriety," Shelly says. "Not being a tourist hub, the residents resented any note at all."

"But I lauded its historic role starting with their Indian massacres and English wars. And named family names because they're among the most revered in American history."

"You know what Joyce said about history," his wife says. The room silences to listen. "You tell them,

Marc."

"No you, Lael."

"Merely gossip?"

"Oh, wild," Paul says to the host when she
penalizes him for leaving early by giving him the
OLD in the "turkey and mussel mold" in plastic wrap.

"Your just deserts haven't jelled yet," she says.

"Before you go," her husband says at the door,
"what letters do we drink?"

"Hello?" Tilly says.

"Um, ah, oh, is, Ez in?" shimmy-shamming a
boy's voice.

Shelly calls. "Need any alkalizers, analgesics,
anything I can bring up?"

"Certainly if I swallowed anything you
brought up I'd feel even worse. Have a lark. I'm
turning in."

"Save it," Tilly says.

"Instead would you accept cables collect?
Smidgeon roast? Sight better? Feliogrim, Til?"

In today's book section a friend's book is
reviewed. The main character spends the entire
novel on the phone with his wife, ex-lovers, parents,
child, agent, editors, telephone operators, Time,
Weather, Information, *Informacion, Reseignements*,
"Nyet: unlistened," Dial-A-Prayer, A-Poem, A-Heart,
A-Disc, A-Steak, A-Date, A-Recipe, A-Message,
A-Surprise, A-Joke and with noble writers he's
never met but calls London, Paris, Buenos Aires and
Moscow for to chat or debate with or chide or glorify,
widows and children and grandchildren of writing
masters who he inquires about and panegyrizes,
friends whose reviews about their books he's recently
read and indirectly despises.

"Who's there?" his friend's son says.

"If I told you would you keep it under your

hat?"

"I have no hat."

"Not even a snow cap, pith hat, fore-and-aft 'at? And point of fact, you think I would've nightwalked my way way past the ionofinal-latterstratosphere to phone from the next planet station to station without knowing who's there?"

"We have no telecommunications with Venus or Mars yet."

"Heavens to jetsy, where's your eccentricness, unconscientiousness, self-deceptiveness, illogicality? You young men of today are all so solemn and earnest."

"Don't tell me what to be."

"Now don't give me any backbleat, kid, or I'll tell your nanny. Or your nanny's Manny. And your nanny's Manny's branny flanny ran he so he might tan thee or use me plan E to can ye fanny down a cranny and then there shan't be any grandstandee, understand me?"

"I'll get Chip senior."

"Who's there?" Chip says.

"Once upon a time it puzzled me why you wouldn't even intimate what the plot of your novel was."

"Rather the reviews, Paul, hey? You said you were only intending to write a short story about phonecalls, though you know everything's up for grabs. And your basic theme's been vastly broadened and revamped, as I've inserted my spouse. Though you still might be trounced for trying to dapple with my canon if you now submitted your piece, as it's getting the notices, disceptations, polemicists left and right and pro and con and on and on and a movie version, book club alternate, *Digest* abridgement, paperback and perhaps a play. I'd write both screen treatment and stage adaptation and hopingly the lyrics if it's made into a musical or television spectacle as some entertainment consortium's taken an option on doing later on. Besides, I've told you four score of my stories myself."

"Nothing either of us could use."

"Cry plagiarized and I'll insinuate it into the story I'm finishing now."

"That's probably what I'll do with you."

"But I said it first."

"You said the word it first? You're the coiner we're to credit for that? Not that but it? Then may I be neologized as the iter of that or is that yours too?"

"Dummy up for this excerpt from a Buffalo review. Maybe not since, and I'm quoting, 'Celine's first nocturnal journal has there been a book more comically horrible and horribly comic, and I daresay not since West's second lonesome heartbreaker a work more empathic of the dread, fear, pain, futility, terror and outright desperation and bale that enslave and are encaged in us all and the improbability of their ever being unmanacled and manumitted or even fleetingly relieved, despite our prodigious technological achievements and maybe, as this novel infers, because of it. Yes, both the hero and villain of this book is definitely technology, and Mr. Diamond is to be congratulated for putting it to us on the line.' That one I've blown up postersize and hung mounted and framed above the drawing room mantelpiece."

"If that's Paul," Bunny says by the phone, "tell him to pick a day for dinner with us this week."

"Duesday, fednay, cursway, spypay, ratursday, shunfray, nonday."

"Operator," Paul says, "I'd like to place a call to a Miss Marguerite Lift on Moss Road, Lynn, Mass."

"You'll have to dial Lynn Information direct

by dialing regular Information and getting the Lynn area code. Then dialing—"

"You haven't the Lynn code there?"

"The directory's out of reach."

"Sometimes it's impossible to get Information at this hour."

"I'll get local Information if you like."

"You're a dream."

"Thank you. Hold on, please."

"Can I ask one thing else? What's a magic telephone?"

"I hope you won't use one of those. Then I'd be an abettor."

"That's what makes horseracing. Anyway, now I know. And you sound very congenial and droll."

"Droll I wouldn't know if it means laughing at your old stable jokes, which I didn't. As for being genial, far be it from me to say around here, but thanks."

"You don't like your work?"

"If you want to talk more, let me take this party and I'll be back.

"You were saying my work? What kind you do?"

"Write."

"Lots of those around here. I know it's more interesting than my job, though I've no complaints. What's to complain? Hours are bad and take-home's notoriously low, but with my background and degree it's the most secure job I'm equal to holding so the best one I could get. And you do get to speak to a lot of people."

"That is what you do."

"Is it ever. All day, blab blab. What's that you say? Ten dollars of your dimes didn't drop in the

93

tray? Let me take your name and address please. Is
Wallakazookie your name, street or city and spelled
with an e e or y or i e? No, I can't return your last
call's lost change with a special release gadget your
girlfriend says we got. I'm sorry for the inconvenience
that you won't have the money now to pay for the
train, bus or turnpike toll. Pardon me if I still must
insist your number's not what you say, but its first
three exchange numerals are flashing above me in
electro-digital lights plain as day. Yes, this is a real
live voice and not one recorded by Ma Bell fifty years
ago. No, I don't know the ball scores, what it's like
outside or if yesterday's skyjacker got caught with the
ransom money today. And more of the same, though
as a girl I loved the phone. Mother couldn't keep me
off. And confidentially, I do have this rare opportunity
to hear undreamt-of stories I'm sure you'd give your
typing fingers for me to tell."

    "For instance?"

    "Let me take this party and I'll be back.

    "Still there, sir?"

    "Was it a party?"

    "A baby that I think kicked over the receiver
and dialed zero. Receiver's still off and I flashed
my loudest signal, but no one's at its home or so far
heard."

    "Is that what you'd consider undreamt-of?"

    "You're spellbound, I can tell. Hold on.

    "That I think was one of your magic
telephoners. 'Playboy Club credit card,' he said in this
his most silky suave cufflinky openshirted voice, and
then 'two three, five eight, seven two, one six dash
one two, sweetheart.' Always around now we get
the big eastern credits. Men calling their old or new
flames or even their wives across country. Or maybe
their hotshot business exec bosses or mammasans in

Western Wallakazakkazan. Hold on.

"The baby's mother then. Finally heard my signaling and said 'Listen whoever you are with the noisemakers, stop waking my baby and me up or I'll dial o for the cops.' I said 'Excuse me, ma'am, this is the operator,' and tried explaining, but she about split my eardrum seam when she hung up. I don't mind. One thing I learned on the job is that one third of the callers are rude and misfits, another third from kind of okay to a T just perfect and the third third either make no sense or for foreign language or garbled speech reasons I can no for the understand, halvah? Obviously the last third can run in a tinge with the first two, but that's around the ratio they're in. Pardon me again. Believe it or not, I'm still working."

"When do you get off?"

"Which third or tinge are you?"

"I'm calling from Mawkuhpuk and if you're reasonably close and quitting soon, maybe we could meet for a coffee or beer."

"Why not coffee in the early afternoon sometime?"

"I leave tomorrow morning before ten."

"I see. Sure, why not? I'm not far. You have to be new or visiting because everyone hearabouts knows the phone building's the first one off exit 2B heading east. I get off at midnight, so you've time."

"How will I recognize you?"

"You'll be there in front or you just collecting decorative tidbits now? I'm not your little Jill who still plays jacks and dominoes, you know, so I don't want to be waiting for nothing."

"My name's Paul. I'm 246 pages tall. I've circumlocutionary hair with an anamnestic hairline. Also a compendious face, amphibolous eyes, euphuistic ears, semeiologic nose, ideographic mouth

when opened, syncopetic when closed. Lineated
forehead, ampersanded eyebrows, period ellipsic
complexion, rubric orotund cheeks, metaphrastic
last draft teeth, bombastic lips, unbowderlized chin,
expatiated neck, allusive larynx, careted chest, wordy
waist, literal back, figurative rear, parenthetic legs,
abbreviated arms, scholastic hands, capsulized fingers,
solecistic nails, concinnated toes and illegible feet."

"Mine's Sandy and I'm large. Let me give you
local info so you can get your Lynn area code."

"Speakink."

"Is Marguerite Lift in?"

"Vent."

"Went where?"

"Called up by her maker if you have to know."

"What's that? Who's this? How?"

"Her landlady who helped vatch over her till
the month ago and also her good friend till the date.
If you're sayink you're a close someone of hers also
I'll get Henry who vas also her beau. He's packink
to leave vhile I help keep check on the poor soul and
tidy up after him and for the new viters movink in.
Heinrich?"

"Yo."

"This is Paul, Henry, a friend of Marguerite's.
What happened?"

"Untranslatable. *Finis*, the *Ende*. 1939-71,
Springfield, Mass. Stemming from a regenerated
heart ailment she first underwent earlier part of her
life. Gone. Like that, poof. Like smoke, stroke. Up.
I think I know of you. Used to call when I wasn't
answering phones then and several postcards of felt tip
drawings of yourself with backdrop settings of your
surroundings and autobiographical captions and word
balloons. And annually a published story markedly
similar in content to the cards, though without the

bounty of being as daring, colorful and concise. So what now, Paul?"

"I luffed her."

"Not exactly a hard news beat, since was there a man adequately acquainted with her voice and personality and face who didn't feel the same?"

"I've lived with her, went dots by her, apart from her could never get her nearly halfway out of my head."

"Post a Valentine's Day greeting to heaven, but I'm still asking—what now? I libed with her with all my *Herz* too."

"We were engaged, quite young. Naturally, she broke it off. I haven't spoken to her in two years."

"We were promised to one another—signed, sealed, whole *schmier* including the delivery, but the baby died of old age. In my judgment that's what principally killed Marguerite, to hell what her specialists say. Last time we talked was in that oubliette of a hospital award. 'Guerity, Guerity,' I pealed, 'I need you, want you, won't let you go.' She said 'Ah, but it's okay, H. I've found Psyche's surcease and you shouldn't be grieved but relieved to see there can be great joy and peace in being taken away.'"

"How long were you two together?"

"We still are and will be once more."

"What did you say she expressly died of again?"

"Poor conjugation. No infinitive. Improper disjunction and syntaxis. Perhaps a first person jussive, positively pluperfect second person feminine intransitive and durative case. Interrogative. Exclamative. Imperative you ask negative or anything else."

"I once followed after her to Europe. Hour before I was to meet her she zoomed a pneu saying she was shoving on home."

"We passed a *gut* Guggenheim *Yahr* in *Stadte*
am Main O Rhine. All day I scholared and wrote,
she whipstitched and loomed. Lamenting and mopey
as she connatally was, she managed to ride out the
chipperest unchoppiest chime of her strife."

"Lamenting and mopey? She was funny,
lively, laughy, dancy down streets she'd, singy up
stairs we'd, cheery and breezy though bones freezed
in our mutual booths, roosts and rests. What are you
talking about?"

"What are you? One and the same. Marge
Lift. You've disremembered or were so young then
you misunderstood. For laughing she sparingly did,
dancing never. Gentle and attentive for sure, but
gloomy, crestfallen, not to such excess where you
shuddered at staying with her, but preternormally
timid, dashed and depressed."

"Trope."

"Story it, babe, store."

"I say it again. And again till you bend. You
must have strong-armed her into that condition or
some other man or men before."

"Theoretically I'm still in mourning, Paul,
besides what you don't know about the behavioral
sciences and psychotherapy."

"Point, you got. Must excuse. But gaff like
yours forces me to flail out for her. Dear Marguerite
in heaven or wherever you may be, may God's goodly
grace or whatever from whoever be forever on thine
and thee."

"Maybe it was you who depressed her
gloom for me. Because what I see now as your main
shortcoming with her must have been that you never
stopped to think. Truth is, she was growing tired of
your intermittent calls and unending interest, felt put

on and upon by them. Truth is, I said 'Who wouldn't?' and she said 'Don't be cruel, Paul's very sweet but green,' yet always agreed."

"She didn't even enjoy my prose poems to her stenciled in indelible on foolscap?"

"World's getting much realer than that, brother."

"I'll believe it when I read it and my mother when she tells me you're my brother. But what about my postcard comicstrip balloons? They didn't amuse her either?"

"Your colors ran. The e's looked like r's and i's like j's. And you never numbered the frames your pictures were in, so we were always confused."

"Left to right, faithfully like English longhand or printed literature, and you had to know where a consonant couldn't stand in for a vowel."

"Hello?"

"Hi, Mom, I call too late?"

"We're both up, watching the end of a movie. Credits say your friend Gil wrote it especially for TV."

"Worthwhile?"

"Kind of labyrinthian, discomposing, though terse and intense. Some parts even make us laugh."

"Want to get back to it?"

"I can talk and watch both. Dad's been a little weak these past two days, but I think it's the heat. I could barely lift him out of bed this morning. And he pished so much I got tizzy and said 'What do you think I am, your indentured cook, servatrix and amanuensis besides?' and threatened to put his urosheath back on. But he still couldn't speak or even scratch out a note or give me a sign that he had some more to make, so right in front of me he went again. I wept when I saw that and feel so witchy now about what I had said."

"Happens."

"He's repeatedly asked where you are. I tell him every other time, but he mostly believes you've garrisoned yourself in your room for the weekend and has actually heard you typing. Only before he said 'Pallo must be hot into another piece, but what and where it will ever get him is a question mark.'"

"How do you feel?"

"Clammy. Exhausted. Even now there's no relief, no breeze. Maybe a waft of one quaterdiurnally, and when it comes Dad and I gaze bedazed at one another it's so outerworldly. And the tent caterpillars, having consumed the backyard, are now parachuting into the apartment and eating my plants. I keep seeing them creeping esuriently across the walls and floor and one before was on Dad's collar, which I had to flick off and unregenrately kill. I feel they'll all of a sudden invade us by the millions tonight, mass-masticating through furniture and clothes and hearty-mealing us. It's a possibility, for they've squandered all their other food sources and if caterpillars also have noses they'll know we've more savorous roughage here than several health food stores. Dad's organically nonchalant about these scouting forecrawlers and mockingly waved a no when I said 'You think we should stick Paul's manuscripts in the safelike icebox?' I know I won't sleep with these creatures lolloping and lunching about and I can't stop their incursions by locking or plugging up the windows, because of the heat."

"Drink some beer. Cut the branches closest to the windows. Which I of course should have done for you before I left, besides buying you a six-pack and a fan. But I also called to say that even moved out of your place I'll come by daily to assist you and give Dad his insulin shots."

"Thanks. Because whenever I needle him I hurt us both. And I'm afraid of hematomas and you know how brave he is about pain. I must be slaughtering him compared to you."

"Any important calls?"

"Your agent. Said to return it to her Eastport home if I think to tell you she called."

"Dad close enough to talk?"

"Don't mention the wetting. Helpful as you are, you do get him agitated at time by being too hard. Drive well. Our loves. Here's Dad."

"Hey, Pop, I'm in Rhode Island at the Bustellis—remember near where we had that cottage two summers ago? People have asked about you. Friends of theirs used to ride by Melvale Road and see you seated in front tearing up the newspapers and shooing away the wind, and they send you their regards. How you feel?"

"Fine and dandy."

"At your last gasp you'll say fine and dandy. Movie good?"

"Silly. Slow. Boring. You could do better. I want to go to bed. But your mother wants to see how it ends."

"What's it about?"

"Politics. Stupid."

"You like politics."

"Too much chasing. Killing. Noisy guns. Unreal. Handsome heroes and gorgeous girls."

"You never complained. You married one."

"But married to crazy American general who wants to blow up whole world? Where will it ever get him? And American senator who stops him shooting off missles and saves whole world? Makes money. You should. Your friend, Mother says. You write junk like that. Could. I wouldn't watch it again, even if it

was by you, but I'd be pleased. And after, you could
do what you want. And later gives up office because
he can't stand pats on back? That's a politician? Lot to
learn your friend and his senator. And later tried by
country for being national threat? A risk? Makes no
sense. Right before. Senator heard his death sentence
over car radio he's in on his escape from praise. Silly.
Public. Not we, who hero-worship him that much
they almost kill him. Tearing off all his clothes
as souvenirs and leaving him in ice cold. His wife
silly. This crazy general. Whoever heard? A lowlife
president. We've had bad, but him? Makes money.
You could. This young senator like college dean who
even his wife and children leave. Scared of association
with him and now he's no place to go. Right now.
'Where?' he says. 'Which way which way should I
take to escape these States?' he says. This moment.
On screen. Play by play, talking himself like he's mad.
Car comes. Watch this. Car his son's in, I see, who
wants to ride over him. Dad ducks into bushes. Nice
family. Up again slapping his clothes. He's going to go
far on this busy highway. By time he's a grandfather
he'll have reached city limits. I'll tell him where to go.
Another profession. Your friend also. But if he has
mouths to feed? But nothing. This picture nothing.
Saw better junk when we got in two for five, anyone
got three? I'd like to go to bed."

    "Tell Mom."

    "Told. Right here. Speak to her yet? Sitting
beside me to see the end. Must've. Because I didn't
answer the phone. But it's all right. She works hard,
goes through a lot. After, we'll have a bite. They
feeding you well?"

    "Very elaborate dinners."

    "No breakfast and lunch?"

    "All I can eat. And four o'clock tea, five

o'clock broth, six o'clock potage and preprandial port and postdiluvial potations."

"Drive carefully and don't think you're so smart."

"Take care, Pop. Have a good snack."

"Bring back fresh vegetables off the stands."

"Hello, Robin. Interrupting anything?"

"No, Paul, I've always time—glad you called. It wasn't important. I had a long discussion over lunch with Erica Gentila about your stories. She said she's been thinking a great deal about you lately and wondered if you ever considered writing a nonfiction article for their magazine."

"On what?"

"You know what they use. Personalities. Controversy. Minor scandals. Sports, war, car, political and financial themes and lampoons on contemporary life, though with a short story organization, sense of discovery and compactness of characterization and detail. I plumbed and pumped her for inklings, but she said if you came up with one she'd be happy to introduce you to the *handlers* who'd handle such a piece."

"She see my last story?"

"That one—*The Plot*? Again your good writing is evident on every page, Paul. But why a woman who just about ends up doubletalking incoherently about how much she loves this man behind a door who never says a word back to her and for all we know isn't there? Is he?"

"Can't even say about the door. I'll make her a man."

"Fine, if you make the person behind the door a woman. The story's selling direction will have to be changed, but aside from all that it's repetitive, needs to be trimmed. You can only run on so long with a runnymouth character like that till we want to shout 'Come on, ma'am, mum's the word or make some move.' Sliced in half it has possibilities, but now I couldn't send it around."

"Sliced in half it'll be four and a quarter manuscript pages and then too brief to be considered anywhere. I'll submit it."

"Work on it first. Why kill the story's marketing potential by submitting it now when it can be improved? And Miss Gentila. She was very concerned about you. Mostly because she thinks you've excellent descriptive powers but feels your talent would be better applied to nonfiction than fiction and I tend to agree. Much as I like your stories, Paul, I think you'd write wonderful articles."

"Operator, I'd like to place a call to a Mister, Monsieur, *Monster* S. Beckett on rue something or another in Paris, France. Actually, I've no title or grounds. Mercy."

"Rose, is Lucia around? We had such an enjoyable talk before I thought we could do it some more."

"She's in the camper, not feeling well. I shouldn't have even come down to take your call."

"What's it, something serious?"

"Hey. It's presumptuous getting anxious over the phone when you can't in any way help. It's only an earache. Painful, yes, but she'll be out extroverting every which way tomorrow morning after tonight's antibiotics do their swell, so don't be unnerving me with your wails, okay?"

"Suspension points."

"You must have a fat roll to make all these calls."

"Last term's teacher savings—want some?"

"No. I've always felt that once a person's

given material things, he resents the receiver and feels cleared of any emotional responsibilities and caring he might have had. And I never felt you were obligated to give and don't want you to feel you are."

"I'd like to. I promise to remain emotionally sniggled and spiked. And you can't have much."

"We're always short. Now we're on Welfare, but it provides. There is one thing it won't take care of that I'd really like to do. Primal Therapy. If I'm accepted they can't take me for a year and then I'd have to have the two thousand to pay for it, money before words. If you care when the time comes, I'd be very grateful."

"What is it?"

"What two of the Beatles went through."

"Next will you be jetting to the Maharasacal's Indian ashcan for a real treat?"

"They did that before Primal—all four. But don't be superficial. Till now you've held and squelched yourself and we could talk."

"My transmigraintion tonight."

"If you've that much money, apply for Primal."

"Have I never given you my views on therapy for creative writers? It mars their handwriting and reduces their typing speed."

"This has to be what happens when someone talks to you two nights out of three. And you say you want to fly out and nestle with us a spell?"

"*Mit* out *mein* hurts."

"And if Lucia wasn't here?"

"Why shouldn't she be? Just the holy family we of us, campering in your damp hamper or in a fleecy triply sleepy caul in the copse. What do you say?"

"Same. A man who left me a year ago and

last month wanted me desperately back. Or my back
desperately. All the same, I was alone. Why, not. It
will probably end with my heart efflorescing and then
picked, pecked-at and scrunched underfoot, 'Keep
off the grass' and 'This vegetation to be regarded not
discarded' signs notworthstanding. Another weighty
relationship fraught with ambiguity and my once
more forsworn against man per se and fi dy till the
sun god Hissel sweeps me off my feet, seats me on his
stick and streaks me to his utility closet. Or the sun
or the sin of the sun god—Hyperbole...Apologue...
appalling. Not now. He's here. In this very room
searing us all marshmallows while his ears roar. You
know I can't leave a man but the reverse. Man a leave
can't I know you? What I'm patiently waiting for is
one who will swear his everlasting love and positive
intentions to me. Would you ever do that?"

"I could."

"You might, as a device, in again out again
win again, but I doubt I could really count on you. No,
though if you do come out here we'll drive down to see
you. Lucia and I. In short, I'd like us to at most remain
friends."

"Senor Borges is not at home," a woman says.

"Is this his mother?"

"If you wish to speak to this lady, sir, rather
than person to person to the party you originally gave,
I will have to start charging you for a station to station
overseas phonecall."

"No no. B and B. What a mixture. Nother
form of menthyl. Thank you all. *Adios, bonjour.* And
lieu too, Soldier Niscien, harry don. Sum five ye."

Two women are in front of the phone
building.

"Paul?"

"Hello, Sandy. Your description was perfect."

"Too large, right?"

"The east of exigent 2B. How do you do?"

"My co-operator, Gail. If you didn't show she would've driven me home."

"Still can. I don't like his looks. Something lurking about him. Round the eyes."

"Don't worry. She's only kidding."

"Am not. Look at them. Bodeful. Stern. Machiavellian."

"Yes, we must get Paul new eyes first, but all the eyestores are closed."

"And his taste in clothes?"

"You skipped his nose bridge and dental work, dear."

"Open your mouth. So don't open. I'll get to them yet. Though my Mary Marvel vision says bad bite. But the clothes. Inauspicious. Malifical. Brown and red. You are a card-carrying charter member of a syndicalistic standpatting bund? And one sandal strap's broke. Oh, you're making a gross mistake, Sandy. Vewy beeg."

"Actual fact is when she heard you were a writer she begged to come along."

"Oh say can you see? On my knees. By the dawn's prematurely early light do-re-meing 'Please, Sandy's feet, let me meet the ominous Mr. Writingman.' Also the aweless one, mayter of factly, since he didn't need a chum to bum along."

"Actual fact two is that Gail and I are writing a mystery book together and got into a snag and need professional advice."

"Depends on what kind of writing he does. If it's fiction—it is? Whodunits? You don'tits? Anyway, I'll stay. Sandy, take my hat and coat. Where in tarnation is my hat and coat? Someone chopped them. I mean my gloves and scarf. Never mind. It's too hot for hats, coats and scarves. But I do have a burgeoning manuscript in my car. Sandy and I are doing alternate chapters of our creepy shocker, though I seem to be the one who's writing most of them."

"It was your original idea."

"You said you'd do every other."

"I will. Keep writing the odd numbered ones and I'll catch up soon."

"How can I write chapter seven when I still haven't six?"

"You did five without four."

"What she wants is for me to write her two undone even chapters and she'll take over from there. You won't get co-author credit if this keeps up."

"Then I'll take back my chapter two."

"Try. I've a copy in the car, one sealed in a closet wall and a third in a Swiss chocolate factory under a special flavor, and grill or pillory me I'll never surrender them all. Though if the book does sell I'll settle with you by giving you the most minimum prorated share."

"I'll sue."

"Who'll you sue? Not me. Sue Sue if you want. By the way, where is Sue? I bet she's the snit who sneaked my hat and coat and scarfed my gloves. Oh, take it then. Not you, Sue—you take a long walk with Will. Because that chapter of yours is a paltry piece of eptnessless as it is. Well, get it, and also my smokes and glasses off the dash. Then we'll go to the Pizzapen and see what he thinks." Sandy goes.

"What's the book about?" Paul says.

"Two phone operators oddly enough like ourselves who hear a murder being committed over the phone and get embroiled in it and solve a number of related deaths. It's called *411*—a play on the eye for an eye and tooth code, which is one of the main motives behind the crimes. Not a play, of course, but a book. And there's even a minor character in it named Hammurabi—my touch: an honest humble handyman who I hope most of the readers will deem the killer because of the title and his gentleness and taciturnity, till he gets his too. Slit. The first chapter takes place in our operators' room in another real state though fictive city—Flint, after my mother's maiden name. Our supervisor's the same also, but in the mystery we make her one of the two masterminds behind the murders who almost kills the ops too. Sandy usually works right beside me on the boards and one night I thought I heard a murder over the phone. A woman called. Said, 'Operator, help, get the police, this man's trying to kill me, this man in my room. He already hit my head with a wrench where I got the scar.' 'Did he do that just now?' I asked her and she said 'No, it takes time for a scar to form—that was last year. Now he's lunging at me with a cookie jar.' 'What's your address?' I said. 'No,' she said, 'he's really my husband and it's only a spat.' 'You want me to get the police or not?' I said and she said 'I don't know.' Then a man got on the extension and said 'All right, hon, you know that's all a lie. Now I'll have to punish you for what you told this nice girl by holding back your fun money and sending you to bed without your hot milk and rubdown and TV. My wife,' he said, 'is a lunatic, Operator, and between us was only family words, so bear her no mind,' and he hung up. 'Is he telling the truth, ma'am?' I asked and she said, 'No, Operator, I mean I don't know, Operator,' and hung up. All well and good. The murder didn't actually happen. Or for a couple of weeks in the local newspapers it was in noways reported as having happened, though as Sandyhead said, that woman could be right now decomposing in their basement or backyard grave with her cookie jar shards. But when I first told Sandy about the call I also said 'Nifty idea for a beginning to a mystery novel, wouldn't you say?' Because I thought what the world maybe needs with all the female attention women's rights has been getting is a thriller-diller disentangled and solved by two coolheaded modern industrious beauties who are perhaps a trifle more splash and exotic than ourselves. That's how we began."

"Here it is," Sandy says. "Unmysterious chianti stains on the top pages, but I forgive."

"Don't forget the two missing chapters, Paul. So besides everything else, you might give Sandy pointers as to how to write them in."

"You going to prorate Paul also?"

"Eeek. You don't prorate someone, dear. You either cut him in equally or apportion to him on the number of chapters he writes or editing help in hours you've estimated he's given and all on an equitable wage scale."

The opening line is "Operator," a woman said breathlessly, "a man's trying to kill me with a knife, so please get me the police."

"Drop 'breathlessly,'" Paul says.

"But the woman I spoke to on the phone that day was breathless. She could hardly speak."

"Gail thinks we ought to start off with dialogue. I think you have to explain things to readers before hitting them with a strange woman's voice."

"A breathless voice, which is ample explanation: something's clearly wrong from the start. The 'breathlessly' stays."

"Maybe you're right," Paul says. "Though if a woman's about to be slashed by someone, I'm not sure she'd be so concerned with politeness to say 'please get me the police.'"

"She says it out of habit. I think it accurately defines her character and past breeding and even her monetary status, as well as the frenzied state of affairs."

"I don't mind the 'please,'" Sandy says. "But the starting it straightaway with a woman's voice I can do without, breathless breathing, breeding or not."

The next line is "Yes, ma'am," the telephone operator at station four said, adjusting her headset and mouthpiece, "what's your address?"

"Just have it read 'What's your address? the operator said,'" Paul says.

"How will we ever get it to mystery-novel length?" Gail says. "Your way would be only one-liners and gives no news as to where they are or what they look like or have on or anything else. Our readers wouldn't know what kind of operator she is or even if she's a she."

"If a woman says 'Operator, a man's trying to kill me,' the reader almost has to assume it's a telephone operator she's speaking to and that most of these operators are still women. You wouldn't say 'the female telephone operator at station four said.'"

"I'll make it 'phone operator.'"

"Make it 'phone operator.'"

"But the adjusting the headset and mouthpiece you still don't like?"

"Too much time between the operator's actual words. People in stories and novels are too often adjusting and puttering with things before speaking— tamping cigarettes, blowing smoke rings, buttoning, unbuttoning, rebuttoning and such."

"But you know, a single or double set of comfortable earphones has never been developed yet. And the mouthpiece is such an unnatural contraption to have in front of your mouth that most of the girls are forever swinging it from side to side to keep from splitting their lips or cracking their rabbit teeth."

"It's true," Sandy says.

"I'm only saying what I'd do in my own story."

The woman gave the operator her address. Then a man came on the phone and said "Don't bother with her, Operator. My wife is a raving lunatic, so pay no heed to whatever she might have said." Then he hung up.

"You could have written exactly what that man told you that day," Paul says.

"I didn't think it would be right," Gail says. "Not only because it rules out any challenge of changing the sentences around and maybe learning something about writing from writing this book. It also wasn't a strange enough use of words for a mystery."

That night, after work, while walking home, Stella and Grace went a mile out of their normal route to check on the address the woman gave. Grace thought she might have made a mistake in not reporting the incident to the police. Or at the very least, to her supervisor, which all operators were supposed to do in cases of questionable emergency phone calls.

The house was dark and seemed haunted. Crows cawed in far-off trees. The lights in all the streetlamps had been knocked out. The neighborhood was completely deserted. All the houses but this one were boarded up. Grace remembered reading in the *Standard Gazette* that this area had been abandoned and its residents relocated for a huge urban renewal program.

Paint peeled from the wooden frame of the house. The front gate hung by a solitary wire. Tall weeds had replaced what once must have been an attractive garden and yard. The apple and pear trees in front of the house were drooping and the fruit was filled with worms. Most of the apples had fallen to the ground and gave off an acrid, pungent odor that the two young women had detected and wondered about when they first walked down the street. The moon was full. The sky seemed curiously portentous for one speckled with so many stars and so bright. A black cat appeared unexpectantly on the chimney and hissed at them before disappearing under the eaves. Stella and Grace climbed the creaky steps to the large veranda. The bridgeboards beneath them buckled and seemed on the verge of collapse. Stella jumped and shrieked when she felt a furry object touch her ankle. It was only a caterpillar that had dropped from one of the many grape vine leaves which wound around the veranda's balustrade.

"Let's get out of here pronto," Stella said, scared out of her wits.

"Not till we've made certain there isn't a woman in there who frantically needs our aid."

They held hands. Grace pushed the doorbell. The bell didn't ring. Stella tapped on the door. "Like this if you want someone to hear you," Grace said, and she really gave it a knock. They waited. Nobody came.

"Well, nobody's home," Stella said with relief. "Now let's go."

"Let me try the door first," Grace said as she gripped the doorknob. The door wasn't locked. She turned the knob all the way and slowly pushed the door open with her fingertips. At the precise moment the door fell loose from its rusty hinges and slammed to the floor in front of it, the telephone operators saw a woman tumbling three steps at a time down the long, curved flight of marble stairs from the second floor.

They both screamed and ran out of the house and back up the street. Bats flapped out of the dark trees they passed and vanished into the night. They called the police from a corner police box. *That*, at least, worked. When the police came they told the young women that nobody had lived in that house since an entire family of eight and their three dogs and a rare tropical fish and bird collection were all butchered and buried in its basement twenty years ago. That case, the police said, was still unsolved.

The police and young women went to the house. The front door was back on its rusty hinges and all the doors were locked. The police jimmied open a kitchen window, but couldn't turn up a corpse or any sign of a struggle in the house.

"I think you girls have been seeing too many television gumshoes," the police sergeant said. His sidekick laughed. Shaky with fright, Stella and Grace asked to be escorted to the apartment they shared on the other side of town.

That night they couldn't sleep for fear they would be butchered in their beds by the same person or persons who slew that large family and all those animals twenty years ago and maybe also that woman they had seen rolling down the long flight of stairs.

"Take a hot toddy and crawl into bed with me," Grace said to Stella. Then, clutching one another for dear life, they finally managed to get some winks in at around six in the morning when the sun was beginning to rise and the sparrows and blue jays could be heard singing and squabbling on the building's front lawn.

"That's chapters one through three," Gail says. "Four's what Ms. Lazybones here could never find the time to write."

"I will—my word. Starting with this Tuesday

when you're visiting your mom."

"What I want is to have the girls return to their four-to-twelve shifts the next day and be scolded by their supervisor for not mentioning the woman's call. Also for cooking up that tumbling-down-the-stairs story to the police and almost causing a big to-do for the company, which could have cost the girls their jobs if the PR people hadn't kept it out of the papers. So they forget the woman's call and body, or try to, and that night Stella was having her doubts that Grace ever received a call from that woman or even that they saw the woman flying downstairs. That, Sandy has to make sound especially plausible, as it isn't easy for a person to suddenly begin claiming she didn't see something which that very same morning had kept them both from sleeping they were so afraid."

"That's why I haven't written it yet. I don't know how to make it plausible."

"You almost can't," Paul says.

"Who's to say," Gail says. "For now we'll keep it out unless we come up with a convincing reason for her suspicions. Because I love the idea of someone doubting what she saw and her best friend heard and saw the very moment she just about gets corroboration of it over the phone. For the voice of the old man tells Stella to get the police quick, help help, that kind of fear and haste, as someone's about to leap at him with a knife. And right after he gives the same address the woman of last night gave, the phone goes dead. Mind you we never for a long time specify what sex it is that lunges and leaps. Stella tells Grace what she heard and Grace says let's not make last night's mistake, and they go to the supervisor. But the supervisor, who's much like our own except for her lacking the considerateness our real supervisor has—"

"She's gotten a lot of girls out of ticklish

situations," Sandy says. "And not just professional."

"In actuality, for in our book she tells Grace and Sibyl—I mean Stella. It only took Sandy seven chapters to decide she suddenly didn't like her original mystery-gal moniker and it still rattles me—all those places I had to erase and Stella I had to type in. Anyway, the supervisor says they're imagining things again and orders them to forget what Stella said she heard over the phone with the old man. 'Fine with us if you accept full responsibility for the call,' Grace says, or something in kind. 'Just so long as the company knows that you know we told you and you don't later go around saying we didn't if it turns out to be true."

"I like that," Sandy says. "Anyone got a pen?"

"No you don't. Now I said don't give it to her, Paul. Start a precedent like that and she'll never write with her own words. So—you both still with me?—the phone operators go back to their posts. But that night, which you can begin reading with my chapter five on this line, they returned to the deserted house. Stella didn't want to go. "It's too dangerous and eerie," she said, but Grace persuaded her: "How else can we ever clear up our employment records for more desirable jobs later on? Because the company's already got it down that we're both incorrigible hoaxers and ingrained cranks and foul-ups."

This time they went to the house armed with anti-mugger mace sprays they purchased in a late-closing drugstore, and two flashlights borrowed from work. The evening was on the order of the one before. The moon was even fuller, the sky cloudless and luminant with stars, though again curiously bodeful in an almost death-omened way. Crows cawed from distant trees, frogs croaked from unseen ponds. The streetlamps hadn't been repaired. This was something

Grace had suggested to the police of the previous evening should be done if they wanted to insure a safe neighborhood, even if only a few scattered relocation holdouts and impoverished squatters lived there anymore and cars never seemed to drive by.

The front gate was off its loose wire again and remained embedded in the thick grass like sea-shouldered driftwood sunk in moist sand. The trees drooped further and the fruit was even more acrid and pungent than on the preceding night.

"Pee-yoo it stinks," Stella said, holding her nose. "More apples must have fallen from today's storm and and

"You have two ands on this line," Paul says. "Was that intentional to express Stella's fright?"

"Where?" Gail says. "No, it was my own typo. But thanks. I think it works."

and and are rotting."

"Shut up," Grace says. "You want to get us murdered?"

They tiptoed up the ramshackle steps to the veranda. A dog, sounding more like a wolf, howled from one of the nearby abandoned yards. The moon was now so bright they didn't need their flashlights. Grace tried the doorknob. Again, the door wasn't locked. Again, she opened the door, pushed it all the way in ever so gradually, and they looked around the enormous front room which many years ago must have served as a combination parlor, dining and living room area. The disturbance this time wasn't the front door slamming to the ground, but a clamoring noise to their right. They flicked their flashlights on and beamed them to the spot where they heard the noise. There they saw a basement door being flung open, the door crashing to the floor, an elderly man stepping over the door and its mounting cloud of dust and limping towards them while shouting "The colonel, the filthy colonel," and just as Stella and Grace were about to spray him with their chemical sprays, the man dropped on his stomach at their feet, his arms and legs splayed, a knife plunged into his back.

"You really can't plunge a knife into a man's back anymore," Paul says.

"Why?" Gail says. "Bone structure there make it unfeasible?"

"It's done too often."

"If he had the knife plunged into an arm or leg it wouldn't kill him. And in his head he'd be dead from the start. And if it's the stomach it's plunged into, he'd have to have limped backwards towards them for them not to have seen the knife till he fell on his back, which would hardly seem the movements a dying man would do."

"Have the knife stuck in his back. Or sticking out of, in his, jammed, rammed, implanted, infixed."

"You make it sound as if he was knifed with a begonia or bribe," Sandy says.

"I originally wanted him to clump up the long staircase," Gail says. "Maybe get gunned down by a bullet when he reached the top and to fall face forward over the banister to the first floor."

"You have a fetish about people flopping over banisters and down stairs. That first woman's fall was her brainstorm also."

"It worked, didn't it?"

"Once, okay, but not every victim."

"That's why I wanted him dropping over the banister to the floor below this time. Something like this. Could you move aside please? Now—I'm sorry, you too, Paul—crack of the rifle or what have you, and he grabs his chest and yells in dying agony 'The colonel, the filthy colonel.' Or he doesn't have to yell, but—"

"The colonel has to be referred to before the man dies," Sandy says.

"I mean it could be yelled, screamed, said, plunged. No, he can't just say it, as how will they hear him down there? You see, I want to give the effect of this really grand enormous room."

"Who's the colonel?" Paul says.

"Aha," Gail says, "getting interested I see. Must mean the book can't be all that bad as you said."

"I never said."

"Well, the colonel turns out to be the—"

"Don't tell him," Sandy says.

"Gworf."

"Do you promise not to tell him?"

"You don't have to stick your hand in my mouth. Yuch. What kind of soap you use, vermicide?"

"Sorry, but I wanted to see if Paul could guess."

"I haven't seen him in the manuscript so far."

"Because our little Sandy sweet hasn't written those chapters yet. But he's there. now, before, and then later in the letter the dead woman got from the colonel which is found in her purse."

"I never read where her body or anything of hers was found."

"No, that comes after," Sandy says. "The girls call the police again and they come and the man's body's not discovered but a pocketbook is. It's the dead woman's from the night before and contains all the normal belongings like money and hairware and credit cards, plus a letter from the colonel."

"A colonel—the rest of his identity's undisclosed. Anyway, he falls like this. Everybody ready? Lights, camera: arm or arms behind back or over a shoulder or not, one hand clutching the part of his body bullet-struck and falling head-first over the banister and making two complete spirals in the air before his skull smashes reverberantly against the marble tesselar floor."

"What is this guy, an aerialist?" Sandy says. "Two spirals. Let's make it three. Why not have him slide topsy-turvy down a highwire on his fingertip or nose? One's plenty. Because how many feet you have him up there where he can complete two spirals before he lands?"

"It's done in movies."

"Stunt men. That's their skill. You see, but do you believe? This man's old and it's a book."

"One, then."

"None. He dies at their feet."

"He can fall from the second floor landing to their feet."

"Either the woman dies at their feet or he does, not both. And since we've already written her as tumbling down—All right, you've written her with the stairs, then he has to pop out from the basement or another room or drop dead before he reaches them. Also, what kind of visual display are you giving us here, splashing his head on a marble floor? A mess. It'd be an ugly mess. Which I wouldn't want to enlarge upon as the chapter's writer or even read."

"It's probably not necessary to go into the gore. Just have him drop to the floor below."

"You too, Paul? Sandy, you're contagious. Everybody get away from her. Et tu, ladies and gentlemen—get your pies to go, and run. And I ate from the same pizza tray as her? No wonder you use vermicide. Someone sprayed it on you. Your father. For with all due respects but in furtherance of urgent reassertion and iteration, how in hell can we finish a nominal-sized book without explicit details? You have to have so many and such such pages for a novel, don't you?"

"About one-fifty for a mystery, I guess," Paul says.

"How many would that be of ours?"

"Yours are sort of short and lean."

"They're eight and a half by eleven—the standard stationer's size."

"But you've sixteen, seventeen lines a manuscript page and about ten words a descriptive line."

"Twelve on this one. Eleven on this. Ten...ten, dialogue...and eleven again."

"Two-fifty of your pages."

"We'll make it."

"This Thursday, Gail—solemn warranty. Like to know the title, Paul?"

"Told him, dear."

"It doesn't only mean dialing Information either. Cerebral Gail thought it up and I believe we owe a standing ovation for the big G, folks. Hip hip. The big C, rather. Hurray."

"Thank you. Why thank you. Each and every other of ya—thhhank you. Mmmm. Mmmm. Mmmmmp. Love ya all."

"How does the book end?"

"Let's see," Sandy says. "You know the police being called and the man's body thin-airing and the pocketbook found on the grounds. The police didn't think much of that clue. Irrelevant, they said. A purse snatcher threw it there."

"With money and cards in it?"

"Then without," Gail says. "Lipstick, hair stuff, eyebrow pencil and the letter. But to the girls this new clue remains—who's the filthy colonel? The only colonels they know, clean or dirty, is the one who runs all those Kentucky fried chicken places and the president of their phone company, who was a semaphore and wigwag wizard for the signal corps in the last great war. But they think it can't be either of those men."

"The president of their company's a very dignified high-principled family man, as our own president is. Who on occasion like our own comes down and asks after the phone operators and how their children and parents and people related like that to them are."

"If you ask me," Gail says.

"He's nice. You've said so yourself. Our real president, that is. With a winning smile and cute curly gray sideburns and an aftershave lotion that every girl in the Hole would use as a cologne if it didn't cost so much."

"What he'd like to use every girl for is another story."

"Maybe that's the one you ought to exploit next," Paul says.

"Yeah, well, in our book we make the smell on his face witch hazel and his sideburns trimmed, dark and snipped an inch above the lobes. Because for all we know he or one of his spies might get hold of our work in progress before we're through with it and dump us before we can afford to be through with them. Or else the book's earning power might be so pitiful that we'll have to keep our jobs."

"What happens after the colonel's letter?"

"They return to work," Sandy says, "and are severely rebuked by the supervisor for the embarrassment they caused the company. Apparently the PR people couldn't hush up their latest haunted-house episode and she tells them one more repeat of this, girls, and you're canned. But that afternoon they get a third call which they listen to jointly. Same thing—another dame. Life and death. Help, murder and police. Same address, she gives, and then the lady's phone is knocked over and before they're disconnected they hear a long tussle and screams and sighs."

"Are Stella and Grace the only operators in the phone building?"

"You mean the coincidence of their being the only two to get calls?" Gail says. "We thought of that, but we'll work it out."

"Why not have a few other operators get some and then telling the girls that the supervisor also told them to disregard the calls."

"Mister, let me shake your hand," Sandy says.

"For that I think he deserves the last slice."

"No no."

"Mind then, San?"

"Seeing how you've positioned your fork prongs over my fingers—no."

"So the novel ends with several more murders. A foot found. An inscribed ring uncovered. Strangers chasing the operators down streets. Through the phone building maze. Phoning to warn them to get out of town. Terrorizing them in their apartment. While they take baths. Trying to poison them and incinerate them and run them down with a car and then a truck with pop-out swords for bumpers and disappearing foreign plates. And their being fired. The supervisor getting them institutionalized as corporate and civic risks. The girls escaping the asylum and being forced off a bus by two torpedoes and into a cab and bound, gagged, hours before they're to be operated on and after which executed for their most vital functioning parts, organs and enzymes of their nervous, labionasal and laryngopharyngeal systems, they meet the colonel and supervisor together. These two, while conducting a scalding and potentially scandalous love affair under everybody's noses, have also been working hand-in-hand like nine Dr. Frankensteins to develop a self-operating and talking telephone machine so they can make a billion dollars from the invention and put a million telephone operators around the world out of work. That's why they lured all those people into the building—so they could use them as human guinea pigs for their brain and voice box experiments. Though all the victims were persons who they also had a long run of grudges against, such as their old grade school teachers, high school principals, physical ed professors, business competitors, lawyers, judges, generals, even restaurant waiters, hairdressers, dentists and moving men. And that's why these two continually got hold of phones to call the operators, as there were hundreds of different kinds of switchboards and telephones in the basement. Some newly invented by the colonel. Others antiques the supervisor used to work with and collected as an operator. But all there to help make one perfectly computerized and automated operatorless telephone that dials, rings, answers, takes messages, ticks off stock quotes, traffic and skiing conditions and racetrack and sports results. Casts ballots and transmits grocery lists to markets without your speaking and plays hours of sweet or classical music or uninterrupted movie soundtracks and stage comedies. Even sets and controls all kitchen appliances and monitors the house against burglars and rings the alarm if you're away or holds conversations for you from its memory bank of your prerecorded speech and breathing patterns and total register of your emotional and mental attitude and responsiveness and beliefs. The book's clincher has a telephone company detective named I. Calvary Coming, who throughout has been given false leads by the colonel and was such a Denny Dimwit that the girls initially suspected him of the crimes, charging to their rescue with guns blazing and doors and windows breaking, moments before the anaesthetized operators were slated to have their tongues removed. We thought the mystery needed more humor than we maybe had given it so far, and for all we know that could be a real man's name."

Shelly's in the studio when he returns. "Alain's passed out and is sleeping it off on the Horner's couch. One last carouse before I sail, Paul?"

"Start anything new since you came?" she says.

"Something fairly long for me."

"Funny, I could never quite get used to you like this. Like this? Like this! I hope it isn't another profound personal drama about your stay here and our lives. Except for your science fiction memoirs—"

"I never wrote any of those."

"You're a writing mill then? Those future and backwards and pre-, post- and renewed revolutionary pieces and soured with society's ills and bolting to the boondocks and living beneath rocks and in caves and hideaways, with no recognizable city, country, civilization, customs, slang or time. Other than for those you were totally unsubtle in disguising who your fictional characters in real life were. Didn't any of these women complain?"

"I always sent them a copy of the story and said I'd withhold or redo any section about them they didn't like. If they bothered to answer at all it was to say they didn't care what I wrote or had published about them. That in my stories they were portrayed as much dumber, plumper, lanker, frailer, tougher, younger, older, curter, crueler, cuter, crosser, coarser and less sensual and selective than they were or are. And that my stories only confirmed their prior convictions that I seldom took the time when I was with them to find out what they and their children and friends were about, and judging from what I wrote, I'd given scant consideration to the question since."

"Well, the cautionary word for today is to be ever so clever, discreet and kind and know your manuscript. Because even now, and by this time you should also know publishers rarely accept fiction where the heroes are writers no matter how unconventional the characters and occurrences are, I feel that while it's doing its interior duties and easements down there it's also probing, memorizing, rhapsodizing, taking notes and collating nuances and compounding whole phrases and pages while trying to tell the true story from the inside. Oh, it's silly I oh, but almost everything about you makes me feel oh, as though I shouldn't be surprised if I got up to it smack close to hear its head going scritch scratch, clitch clatch, clickety clackety, space bary, click click click."

Paul tries to remember the dream he just had. In it he was sitting at his New York desk in the home he and Tilly and Ezra shared for three years in California, writing the story he's currently writing about Shelly and himself. His brother John entered the room. John's been turning up monthly in Paul's dreams and began doing so about five years after the single-seat plane he was in disappeared over a jungle and was never found. Paul asked John if he'd done any writing since he was away. John said "Quite a lot, but I haven't let anyone see it and for the time being I won't be sending it around." Paul didn't speak about the feelings he's recently had that John's writing will turn out to be much superior to his own. He did say "One language can never seem to support two brothers of a close age range as serious writers, and maybe that holds for the world as well. When it does become known that you're alive, I'm sure magazine and book editors will come banging on your doors to get you published, while with me after so many years of a thousand submissions and few acceptances and no notoriety, it'll be the other way around. I also think how silly the stories I've written about the impact and aftereffects of a young man whose idolatrized writer, doctor, sculptor, composer brother was lost on a bomber, space module, blimp over a desert, rain forest, mountain range and canoe in a canal will seem to readers now that you've reappeared and your writing becomes known. Where have you been for ten years?" John said "How are Sis and the folks?" shook Tilly's hand and patted Ezra's head as he left the room. During the entire dream Ezra stood beside Paul, his cheek pressed against Paul's thigh while his arms were wrapped around Paul's leg even when Paul was crooked over the desk correcting his story or striding across the room to greet John. Ezra looked the same as when Paul last saw him three years ago, Tilly about ten years older than she is, wearied, scrawny, captious, mordant, lined, riled, severe. She was with her new boyfriend who was squat, hirsute, jumpsuit, shaggily bearded and nattily haggard and he seemed cynical of Paul and every so often said "Bah" or "Ah" and busily scribbled in a notebook part of a story he'd been writing. Ezra never loosened his hold on Paul's leg, his sad silent face forever gaping forlornly into space. Tilly's parting words to him were "So nice to see you again, Paul, and wait till you read the love story I've written and is being published about you." "Send it to me when you get the galleys," he said and went back to his editing, thinking why should he finish this story when no doubt Tilly's and her boyfriend's stories will also prove to be much superior to his own. Without taking his eyes or pen off the page he placed his hand on Ezra's head. "My boy..."

Shelly calls and says "Would you be a real sweetheart?" and gives him the New London address where he can pick up the boxes for her mattress and box spring. "She's got two of the right strength, size and length and is waiting for you now."

OUT TO LUNCH

"I'd like a coffee black"—"No sugar?"—"Just black"—"Then say coffee plain"—"Coffee plain"—"Anything with?"—"One of your Go-O-Donuts"—"Which one?"—"What've you got?"—"42 kinds, they're all up there"—"Just plain"—"Midget or king?"—"Is the midget very small?"—"You ever see a midget tall?"—"But the king's not too large?"—"King's of normal size"—"Then give me a king plain"—"One coffee plain and plain king" and later as he's lugging the boxes out of the moving van store he sees a man in the parking lot about to puncture one of his tires with an ice pick. "Hey, stop."

"Why? This's my job." On the wall in the lot that Paul assumed was shared by the store, since the side of its one-story structure also faced it, is a sign saying Parking Members Mignolo's Workingmen's Social Club Only. Violators towed away at full Expense to owners and Full Extent of LAW. "Couldn't be clearer. Next time you're not stopping me, as too many drivers take advantage."

"Can't be a next time. I live in New York and am only doing a friend a favor with these."

"Always another story. But if you're thinking those cartons in your van, you best be folding in the sides and halving them."

Paul tries, fails, he shows Paul how. When they get the boxes in the bus Paul offers to buy him a beer.

"No clauses against guests," he says and they go in the club, his arm around Paul's shoulder. "How come I always knew you were an S.O.B. and on my side?"

"Hi, Bart...Hey, Hack," two men say.

They sit at the bar. "You look like a writer," the man called Bart and Hack says, "and first round's mine if I'm wrong." He's a working man but was a writer. "You wouldn't believe looking at my face and talk. Never published much but some crafty stuff in fartsy moccasins run by dildotantes and their richy itch sirens. Packed it all in. Couldn't stummy the dejection blips and their no to nonsense comments and those nasty parties with fifty writers and their wives and some versa verse. And those two fruity businessmen's lunches with my agent and slinky gal eddies that got me nowheres last but blusterously helpless and dovey and whacked when I should've been home working, and the extra early eve blues that I've been whittling away my warful wife and wile while writing these past years. 'But you'll make it, you've got it in you, just keep on plugging,' my agent kept plying, a deary name who swore fame and fortune's right around the corner, Bart, but try as she might she couldn't peddle but those few piffling things and even these she said weren't worth one-tenth the time she was putting in to introdu he is who and seal and send them.

"Born on Manhattan's West Side. Age six, poppa absquats and skedaddles and soon's presumed dead. I wish I was a believer so I could meet my sweet momma in heaven. I remember the ruler-welding Mr. Meany in P.S. 87. The clattering crutches of sock-em Doc Burnsey at No Witt Clinton High. Com lit degree at CCNY. Married at 23. Flanked yanks for us army. Laddie a biby girl. Wife whisked off

with my potboiling best pal, who she also waved a
higher quality lay. Words, turds, good to employ, toy.
Married against. Saintliest girl in the whole buddy
whirl who ever perished from a read dizwheeze.
Wrote radio plays, movie scripts, rhymed epics,
novelettoes. One about a writer who wrote all of
those plus a long story like the one I thought the
finest I wrote about a writer who spends the entire
piece speaking to a couple dozen people on the phone
including a writer who's written a short novel that
he calls a long short story about a writer who spends
from beginning to end of it speaking to people on the
phone. Even essays on the high waters of Faulkner
and low boarders of Venice and Montreux goiters of
Lord Chest and the future of comedy and comedy of
tragedy and tragedy of future and the tragic future
comedy or was it comic tragic future or future comic
tragedy of fiction in general but writing in the long
haul, and one titled Geez but the Beaubreeze and Bees
Me Sees in the Leaves of the City's Ailanthus Trees.

"Stopped writing for good at 42. 40 was the
cutoff date I set for myself at 35, which was the cutoff
date I made at 30. When I hit 40 and was still storying
with no windup in sight, I said make it an odd 20 years
of hard knocking, which is teeming time for a man
to find himself or be found in any one field or even a
littoral wasteland, so I gave it two more years. How'd
I end up here? Stepped off the obligatory freighter
every writer wroth his mirth of my gen took after his
compulsory self-exile in Paris, where for three years
I came to know no one but my landloan, bistro own,
street *poules* and other writers with fixed cutoff fates,
and had a night's final flung. Following aft I thought
hell, here's a place where they don't bounce you out of
bars or bunk you into jugs when you get rip-roaring
stinko and a flophouse's to be had on the same street

you get soused out on. So I pawned my rapatighter, got me a cheap night-to-nighter, then a job, flat, wife, hack, son, house, television, mouse, washing machine, second cab, spankier home, dishwasher, another cab, even more posher, stereo, motorbo, sea and snow skis, these in that order and somewhere in there this club membership and lately its vice-presidency, chars being organizer of the yearly clam fry and keeping the lot clear of unauthorized cars. Man with a pick I've become, though as a writer you can imagine I gave one and all scads of respect and an endless ear for listening, for to me everyone and especially the whiniest grimiest wino had a yawn I could maybe scrawl.

"To me now they're all rotters. Young men with string beards and weird beads bug the crud out of me. Women with braless spluttering breasts and minishorts and what seem like maxilusts are asking to be bopped down, hopped on, popped in and be dubbed used douche bags forever after. All rags but the ones mirroring my hardassed middle views and biases I want to ash-reduce and scatter. I never read books but the factual ones anymore and these chiefly on woodwork, world wars and what few there are on hack owning. I've grown to hate the word fiction, even if once or twice some nights out of what curiosity's left I'll try my hand at it, but nothing comes out but canned rubbish and yesteryear's leftovers. Even if what I now wrote I judged the best work I've done, I'd junk it. Because not taking it seriously anymore was the smartest move I made regarding writing. Just as saying it was the smartest move I made might be the best way of not taking it seriously anymore.

"Because what's fiction anyhow? An illusion produced by illusioners so publishers, agenters and hucksters who know it's a crock of crap can make gobs of simoleans from mobs of bimboleans. Or else

it's a story or novel written by pathological liars
for pathological escapists so neither group can ever
discern the most basic truths and workable realities
about their lives and life. Or it might be masturbation
in public and then swearing on mended knee before
that same public one's utter innocence and absolution
from that anti-social act. If not that then it's at least
childish nonsense elevated by eloquent switches of
phrases and turning of pages to adult meaningfulness.
Though really it's a bunch of repetitious bull created
by society's most skillful repetitious bull artists so
they can call themselves creators and in fact feel they
deserve to make a living out of their creativeness and
creations by telling the same stories of creativity in
diverse ways so it won't reek of repetitious bull. Or
the same story with only slight variations of names,
dates, places, events and titles if bull's what the
publishers assess from their salesmen's reports that
readers will buy or repetition's what readers believe is
inclus- and reflect- and indicative-ive-ive of our up-to-
the-min times.

 "But why go on? Not with my windbagging
and pettifoggery but your own writing. Because
you married? Ever been? Have a child then? So you
know. Kid gets sick you don't want to be sticking it
in a seedy hospital and have it worked over by reject
medics and defective machines. Maybe if I had had
the income I have now the first marriage could have
made good or the second wife would have been saved.
But she was a writer's wife through and true and
reveled in the sacrifices and delusions of my grind
and therefore the false front and beggarliness of our
lives, so she'd seem ridiculous to me now and to her
I'd be one Simon Legreed and turntail fraud. For 'Dear
the day will come' she used to say too. Crowing my
work was greater than the greats. Pridefully dropping

my fiction off and picking it up at publishers and
magazines. That soon—'Oh soon you'll see with me it
will all be worth the stumbling stones and lucubrating
groans and penury, my dearest, songsmith, bard,' she
the defter fibber, yarner of darns. Because for both our
sakes she should have tried snapping me out of it, not
that I could have been roused. Writers as I was are
always asleep so to speak, eyes ever ope, hearty hinds
of hope—is that why she didn't? that wasted soul.
Only Himmler in heave-ho knows. Third wife's all
right—not one for a writer but better than most for an
honest workingman. Each time she sees me making
with the pen she says 'I thought you gave up that
goofery long ago,' and I tell her I'm only practicing
my signature because the bank's returned some checks
I wrote as possibly counterfeit. Daughter from the
first I never see, though I read where she leads the
jolly degenerate wife of a well-heeled Hollywooden
gag writer. 'Writing runs in my blood,' she said in a
recent interview, which was mainly about my 11-year-
old grandson who supposedly wrote most of the lyrics
for this new successful rock and roll skinshow. The
present two children are dull, unimaginative and with
all the prescribed dislikes and likes of their predictable
friends and schoolmates and with no artistic talent
whatever, which I pray will stay with them through
old age and become engraved in their genetic code.
Between us we've two hardcovers, both cook, a few
mass paperbacks, coloring books and follow the dotted
lines for the children, and one apiece on crochet and
macrame for my wife, and that's our library, when
before I was Alexandrian. I've been hacking for a
dozen years and still love driving. Take in more in
a month than an analogous five years of writing.
Have an eight-track stereo I never listen to but the
kids do so they think I'm a Jim dandy daddy. A color

TV and video tape recorder because I like lots of my own reruns and innocuous evening viewing. If I ever talked literature with my wife or the guys here I'd be scoffed out of her considerable affection and my vice-presidency. And what would I blabber on about, since all the books I once loved to discuss I've long since forgotten. Except *Moby-Dick* and Dickens' Dave, though maybe because I've seen those two movies so often. And *The Idiot The Stranger*, as I used to feel both those borderlines were moderately correlative to myself as the morose lonely undervalued and depreciated writer ready to commit any ignominious act or homicidal defense to get myself understood and published. Know where all those books are now?"

"Lost or sold?"

"Retrieved from lang syne friends a decade ago and burnt in a July 4th beach bonfire, the annual night we're legally allowed one. And all my manuscripts?"

"No idea—the same?"

"Good Christ, man, if you don't know I don't see how you expect me to. That makes no sense. Clodly misfired trite old joke. That's also what I've become. Not a trite old joke but teller of ones. Seller of puns. Speller of puns. That's more like it. P-u-n-s. There, you see? What a lunk. Let me stand you to another draft. That makes more sense. And listen, you park here anytime you please. Any dumb mug like myself comes at your tires with ice picks, you tell them Hack the second V.P. said it's all right. You hear that, Skip?" to the bartender. "This kid can park here anytime he likes."

"You and Shelly been sleeping in this room?" Alain says as they push the mattress into the box.

"No."

"It's a question I had no intention of ever asking or even contemplating again and here I might regret having asked it for all my life."

"Don't be silly. Though it would be interesting to know what you would have felt or done if I had said we had."

"That's a question I would never answer and would never expect you to if the same foolish question had come from me."

"Funny, but Shelly once said something to me almost exactly like that."

"She once said that you here and I?"

"No no. Just that some couples after a long time together tend I think to tell the same stories or make certain statements and rebuttals and ask questions with similar wording, articulation, gestures, stresses, interjections and placement and duration of pauses."

"I don't think so. But my advice for us both recommencing with today with what we say is to be ever so clever, prudent and kind?"

The boxed mattress and spring are lashed to the roof of Paul's minibus. Shelly's to drive to New York with him for her orthopedic appointment and meet Alain there at their apartment tonight. She kisses Sharon goodbye.

"Write."

"By the time my letter reaches you you'll have flown to Paris with your *papa*."

"Telegram, then."

"The telegraph people are on strike throughout the non-Sino civilized world."

"Call. And my regards to Willy le Goat and *ma petite grandma*."

"Take my word," Alain says. "If ever your husband moves anything of yours again, it will be your next one, not me."

A half hour out of Mawkuhpuk Shelly says

her back will never be able to endure the bumps of the ride and inelasticity of his front seat and would he please return home?

"Lie flat on my bed in back."

"It's for the same reasons that I was willing to undergo six additional hours in New York and my carting these crates to Paris that I'd resist resting on that thin slab of foam on a slim board you call a bed."

Alain says "One of you have left your manuscripts behind?"

Shelly says "I expect you on the ship at noon, Paul. You'll have two hours to help me along if Alain has demanding business work, and I'll bring the champagne for the peanuts and toast."

At a stop sign in front of the post office Paul sees an unoccupied doubleparked car rolling into the main cross street. He sets his hand brake, jumps out of the bus, into the moving car, steps on the floor brake as he pulls up the hand brake seconds before a car coming from the cross street would have smashed into his side. He releases the brakes and rolls with the car till he's across the street in a corner parking lot. A woman runs out of the post office and says "You, say you, that's my car, get out of there, leave it alone."

"Your car was rolling and I stopped it."

"You were stealing my car and I stopped you. If I didn't think you worked for the Bustellis I'd get the police."

"I stopped your car from hitting another car. Besides saving it from being demolished, the family in that car could have been killed."

"What's wrong, Spring?" a woman holding a dog says.

"Why Eve, hello. This young man was in the very act of making off with my car when I caught him. I think he's with the Bustellis."

"I wasn't and I'm not."

"I saw you walking and talking with them."

"I don't know who they are. So maybe that day I was accidentally walking alongside them."

"I also said talking."

"That's right, she did."

"I have asked people in this village for directions."

"And who by the way said day?" Spring says.

"A good point."

"I meant day as today, yesterday, day after day, of grace, reckoning, atonement and dash the Lord."

"I'd get Chief Ilson to handle this, Spring."

"And why are you so adamantly defending the Bustellis when you say you don't know them?"

"I hate seeing blameless people dragged in so unsympathetically."

"Yes, I'd definitely get Ilson," Eve says.

Paul climbs into the bus.

"Run away if you want, young man, but I have your license number. You're in hot water Mr. GH6218 New York State."

"I think he must be with the Bustellis," Eve says. "I heard they're shipping a corrective bed to Paris aboard the *France* and what he has on his roof looks like a bed."

Thirty miles from New York he picks up its one listener-supported radio station.

"New job as a technical writer."

"Tell us about the poem before reading it," another man says.

"I was living in Houston during an extremely emotional period in my life. My lady was leaving me and my son felt I was deserting him and to make do I had to take a job with this billion-dollar-a-year supplely smooth aerospace firm. New job as a technical writer."

"Did they also manufacture weapons and munitions and minutial cookies like military missles?"

"Systems for weapons. Very sophisticated materiel. Infrared bombsights and rifle telescopes that sought out the day enemy around street corners and the night one by his body smells."

"Then it also must have been a very emotional experience professionally."

"It was. But as you know from your own smithing of verse, any dismal to disastrous situation acquits itself if you reap from it just one gratifying poem. *New Job as a Technical Writer.*

"I'm in this world of rockets and boosters and telemetry

"and ways to descend on the moon with a hush

"and elliptical orbits and tracking and command

"and systems and subsystems and software and stuff.

"I'm praising these programs, I'm being paid money

"my life is as simple as that.

"Dear love where I left you, my child where I kissed you,

"I'm lost in a world of space."

"I like that. Out of your smithy you forged fire."

"I wrote it in my office. My proposals department colleagues kept peeping past the door and saying my, how they never saw a tech writer working so hard."

"That's rich. Precisely what they'd say. Would you mind reading another, and again telling us about it first."

"I was at Fort Meade working as a secret writer for N.S.A."

"National Science or Students Association?"

"Security Agency. I encoded and enciphered, though I'm not allowed to divulge even that much to anyone unto eternalday."

"What will they do, hurl themselves through the station's doors with knives betwixt their teeth?"

"They could, you know. They'd be sanctioned."

"Sometimes I really wish this program was pretaped."

"It was when my lady was bousing down booze and kill pills for the third time in a month and I'd gotten my current girlfriend pregnant. And with this disgraceful job and my son censuring me like crazy again and my friend keeping me up with her cramps, I didn't know who or where the fuck I was."

"Oley."

"Ice cus ex fawn eight sax bel lay gee yea four ofar five Q T N S A twice twice thrice. That's not only its title but a cryptogram that's decoded in the poem's last line. Roughly translated it means—"

"You don't think by the poem's end we can decode it ourselves?"

"Not unless you have one of the three identical codebooks in the world. Need me when I most needlingly nee you, knave God, and as much as we, knee-deep, need thee."

"Knave God? Go ahead. I like it already."

"*Ice Cus Ex Fawn Eight Sax Bel Lay Gee Yea Four Ofar Five Q T N S A Twice Twice Thrice.*"

"By Bob James."

"Just B. James now."

"Excuse me, sir," the dockman says, "But

could you come back in an hour so yours also don't get lost? We're very loaded up now and by then we'll have a lot of free men."

He watches the bus while he has coffee in a diner. In the time it takes to hurry in and out of the bathroom and pay his tab, the top box is gone and most of the ropes around the bottom box have been cut or unknotted and unwound.

"Anyone see any men or perhaps some boys walking off with a box the same size as this one?"

"Nope."

"Not me."

"Nuh."

"Sorry."

"He say docks?"

"Locks, locks."

"Locks like in flocks or phlox?"

"A box."

"What kind of box?"

"Anything in the box?"

"Looks too heavy a box to lift if that one's the same size"

"I think he said the same."

"Did he also say nothing was in the box?"

"What did you say about a box?"

"This box."

"Whose box?"

"His box."

"Like that box?"

"You see another box?"

"No, I meant like *that* box?"

"No, another box."

"Come on, what about the box?"

"Says some kids stole it."

"He knows they were kids?"

"Must've seen them I guess."

"A little kid's going to steal a box that big?"

"Okay, *he* stole it."

"Maybe the kid only stole something in the box."

"He said the whole box."

"He's lucky the kid didn't take both boxes."

"His tires."

"The whole bus."

"You forgot the street."

"If you left a tank out in this town they'd steal the turret."

"The whole tank."

"Where would they put it?"

"They'd find a place."

"What would they do with it is a better question."

"Don't even ask."

"I'll try not to even think."

Paul opens the box and sees it's the mattress he needs. He delivers the box spring to the dock, at a bedding store asks for its cheapest 60 by 80 inch mattress.

"Earliest delivery is Saturday between nine and twelve."

"I need it now."

"Sleep on a bedroll on your floor till it comes. My niece did it for weeks at my sister's when she didn't even have to and said her posture permanently improved."

"It has to be on a ship leaving tomorrow."

"What can I say?"

"And what's what you just said."

"What do you mean what I just said?"

"What do you mean what I just said you just said, but what rather than what's what you said right before you said can I say? But take no note. It's only how a character I recently wrote about spoke and dither makes me doodah. If you said 'What's this?' he'd say 'This's called what's?' But you have no 60 by 80's for me now?"

"When this article of yours comes out I want you to let me know so I can read it."

"Not even a mattress an inch or two shorter or wider?"

"Everything's delivery. And if it's C.O.D. you have to be there when it comes."

The manager of the bedding store 40 blocks north says Paul can have the 60 by 80 floor model but he has no box.

A moving van store acrosstown has a box.

Paul gets the box, the mattress, the manager helps him slide the mattress into the box and seal it up.

"I'll have to charge you three dollars extra for this roll of very first-rate adhesion Danish plastic tape."

"Nick of time," the dockman says. "If it wasn't for a fortunate foot accident, I too wouldn't have been here to stay. Don't ever let the dockers know, but you'll have to assist me with this onto the ship. What is it you have in here, a grand family of stowaways?"

Beautyrest, Shelly said. "That's the one vital item of comfort besides erasable paper which can't be purchased in Paris or anywhere it seems but in the States. What do you think, Paul, an embargo has been placed?" A Beautyrest would have cost him twice as much.

"You look frazzled to the marrow," his mother says. "Let me fix us both a cold gin and tonic to drink."

"Sit and have supper with us," his father says.

"Your mother's making innards and onions and if there isn't enough I'll be thankful for frank and eggs."

He moves the rest of his belongings to his new apartment around the block. His landlady's sweeping the gutter in front of the building. He tells her his livingroom window can't be opened and the downstairs buzzer for both third-floor apartments ring for both third-floor apartments and his tick-back bell to the vestibule doesn't work."

"Life is nothing but arithmetic," she says. "What's good for you one day may not be good for you ten years after that. My husband. He was the senior accountant for the International Container Company and he said your best thoughts are in the morning. You might not believe that now, but think about it later on. There's Jules, your super. He's in my will. Everybody who has been generous and thoughtful to me over the past 81 years is in it, except most of those who are buried or inurned or dead. Your window carries a bad draft from the park, so seven years ago I had the frame nailed to the molding and sill. The rent was fifty-two dollars and four cents, half of what I could have charged then. The previous tenant, Mrs. Kim, couldn't climb the stairs anymore. She didn't complain, since if there was a second-story man in the next building's same-floor apartment, it would mean he couldn't get into yours. Duplicate keys. I'll have to travel downtown to get them early next week. See, what I think is if a person is bad luck to you three times, don't mix in it again. But you have an old-fashioned New York landlady, and I take the Sixth Avenue train to the same expert locksmith Mr. Rockefeller does. Though being a small man with no connections or political power, they took his store away when they put up those hundred-story trade centers and won't give him a cubby hole in either of them, though they promised. Poor man. You're a writer so you ought to be writing this down. The common people who suffer from the powerful, avaricious and rich. Nameplates. What do you think they are but your name punched out in black and then wiped across in chalk and blown, wh, like that, and your letters are forever whitened in. Now that's technology. Should I have him stamp in yours one m or two? Look at that man. Without a shirt on he must be very hot today. I'm practically freezing with a winter coat on, as summer though it might be, it can't be considered warm. Your buzzer works for 3A and 3B only. Now, what I think is that there are callers of other tenants who ring all the bells. If I were you I'd run down to the door and see what this is all about. You don't have to open the front door to the vestibule—a voice carries through. I know that some callers don't like to ring their friends on the top floors to come to the front door as it's such a tiring walk down. So please let me know what hours and kinds of people they are. You can reach me as I'll always reach you—five successive rings on the vestibule bell, that's my sign. All the tenants have their individual bell signals, but they know five is me and five to me is one of them. This is a safe and quiet building, and Mrs. Kim—oh look," her finger following a moth flying between their chests and twice around her neck and hairnet and away—"that's a moth. She seldom had callers. And Mr. Bierson, the previous tenant of 3B. He once said his first comprehensible spoken words were 'Oh father, you're acting so dourly today,' though in Swedish. Well, he seldom was at home as he worked nights, so nobody ever came to his apartment to bother Mrs. Kim in 3A. I don't know if the new tenant in 3B works nights, but it would be a good idea to make sure that one of you does. Those sanitation men. Look at them throwing their cans in the big machine, and so late. I used to have burlap bags from Bengal before any of the brownstones did, but in they went, garbage and all. I'm feeling very sad today, Mr. Clay, so listen to my story. One of those men. He was emptying our garbage into the back of the sanitation truck and leaned over too far and fell in. Pardon me for laughing, but try as they may they couldn't find the man, so he was never found. Arithmetic to ashcans. I've certainly come a long way. How to live somebody else's life in three easy chapters. But if there is ever to be a real story about life, maybe that's what it should be called."

Moved, he puts his father to bed, sees that his pills and intercom sub-station to his mother's master are in reach of his hand, makes for the Liberry, hears fire engines, runs down the block, the building the Liberry's in is on fire, flames but mostly smoke issuing out of top windows and roof, water filtering through four stories into the bar, wood, plaster and glass dropping and spattering on sidewalk, parked cars and street. The Liberry's bartender and a few of its evening regulars are drinking beers from paper bags in front of the bar across the avenue which has been set up as an emergency Red Cross station. Spotlights light the burning building as the firemen work.

"No, look," someone shouts. "There's a cat up there."

"Where?" "Left." "I don't see." "You blind?" Many in the crowd ask and others point to a window ledge on the fifth floor where a cat's perched. "Don't let it fall." "Save the cat." "Cats'll rather jump than choke." "Firemen. You firemen up there," several people shout in unison to the three firemen five flights up on the highest ladder rungs of the hook and ladder truck, the two bottom men grappling and all but subduing the twitchy to jolting hose for the third who directs the jets into a smoldering apartment four windows away from the cat. "Nail it. Bag it. Catch it before it leaps or dies."

Yays, told-yas and applause when a fireman from inside the building grabs the cat off the ledge.

"Ten to one he leaves it up there."

"No, they'll bring it down some way."

"You think one of them's about to trot up and down four floors in a fire for a cat?"

"Only the top floors are affected."

"Then why they breaking all the windows in the first, second and third?"

"You people. More worried for a cat than those three brave men."

"Cats are as brave as people and just as good."

"Braver. Better."

Paul goes to a bar a few blocks away. The streets reek of smoke, new ashes hang above his head.

"Where will all the Liberry customers drink now?" Mickey says. "Kitabi. The script gal. The court steno and college registrar. And the file clerk, pollster, palmist, folio sewer, logodaedaly-dallier and what was his name the pharmacist-notary?"

"Paul and Mickey," a woman says. She once said her name was Pierian but preferred to be called Poem and was known at the Liberry for her yoga exercises on the bar while she sang and composed advertising jingles out of Haiku and triolets. "You two too? It's like a wake. I bet most of the pub shows. Will watered-down beer wash out the stink from my eyes or make them seethe more? There's Sugar and Dawn. Everyone I bet. Oh do I wish I'd stolen all those unduly-bound books off the shelves when everyone always said don't."

To get to the mensroom which used to be

gotten to by elevators he must go through the bar's rear entrance into a hotel lobby and follow the green arrows to the service stairs and down a half flight and along a shadowy lit basement corridor past a forrent tonsorial parlour and shoeshine stand for eight feet and four behinds and down a full flight of stairs and along an L-shaped tapered passageway that ends at two juxtaposed rooms of many urinals, marble washstands, brass fixtures, etched mirrors, hat racks and oak stalls. If he were writing a scene where a man's suddenly alarmed for his life late at night in a vacant subbasement of a once grandiose hotel gone rank and shoddy, he'd set it down here. In a notepad he retraces the route he took from bar to mensroom, describes the ornate rooms of mosaiced walls and inlaid floors and painted ceilings of bathing naiads and ogling fauns, leaves and sees a man sitting on a shinestand chair, lustrous stubbed riding boots on the foot pedals, flared suede cuffs, leather pants, silk shirt, black borsalino hat lowered to his nose, hand-rolled tobacco or marijuana cigarette in his mouth and hands patting the side pockets of his ankle-length raincoat on this muggy clear night. "Match?"

"I don't smoke."

A second man in a different-colored raincoat and identical hat blocks Paul as he continues along the basement corridor. "Money?" he says. The first man cramps in behind Paul and says "I'm here."

"Yes—some." He puts the pen and pad in his pocket.

"Let's have the pad. You could have your bigger bills between the pages instead of pressed leaves."

"Just take the money," Paul says. "Then only the wallet and pen, but leave the pad behind."

"Stay put for five," the first man says, clapping

Paul's throat with the broad side of a stiletto blade, then both dawdling upstairs while flipping through wallet and pad. "Anything there?" "Nothing much— what you got?" "Light's too dark." "Cheap welfare hotel." "Hey, fix on this." "What's he scheming to, rob the bootblack?" From the subbasement floor the roar of two rooms of automatic flushing urinals flushing.

"Perfect." On his wrist he writes th roar from th subbasmnt fir of 2 rms of autmtic flushg urinls flushg

He stays, remembers a similar incident in San Francisco three years ago that he later put in a story. But that was during the day, May, month before he left, walking through a small park squared by the city's finest club and mansion, and a man waved from a bench and said as he drew near "Hey, friend, wait, friend, I know you from somewhere, aren't you somebody artistically famous?" and while trying to place Paul's face while Paul was saying the man's made a whale of a mistake, he stuck the point of his penknife against Paul's ribs. Paul edged back, said "You must be kidding, this can't be happening, I won't, don't believe it, I'm living my own previously published short story," and walked away while the man yelled for him to come back, "Now you come right back here and give me your money," and returned to talking to two ladies on the bench.

Paul tells the night clerk he's been robbed in the hotel basement.

"Nobody's supposed to be down there after six."

"But they haven't a mensroom in the bar."

"Tell them to build one, but we're not responsible."

"In the meantime there isn't a toilet there

and I suggest your basements either be patrolled or locked."

"What if people in the lobby or bar need a mensroom, where you want them to go?"

Paul tells Mickey and Pierian what happened and that one of them will have to buy his next beer.

"I'll pay for it," she says. "I always wanted to feel like one of the boys and I can't think of an easier way how."

"Buy mine too?"

"Only Paul's. I'm not a sucker."

Mickey jiggles his eyebrows. She says to him "How old did you say you were?"

Escorting her home, she says to Paul "May I see your new apartment? I love places that haven't been worked or slept or even eaten in yet. It only exists once, so it's like the smell before the gush, the tremors before the rush, the pandemoniac emblazonment and swirling indeterminateness before a tameless event. Quick. For two pence. Who wrote that?"

"Take my glasses off for me, please?" she says.

"Can you still see the room and me?"

"Where did you put them so I'll know later on?"

He guides her hand to her glasses on the end table, she shuts the light.

She says "We. We. Oh we. I say we. Say we. Sweet we. Love we. Now we. Oh we. Oh we. Oh we, Paul, yours Paul, mine Paul, we."

He says she reminds him of Molly Bloom making or recollecting love and she says "I know. I've been told that by a couple writers and also a literature professor who said I sound as Ophelia might sound if Ophelia had made love."

"She hadn't?"

"I think he said some scholars say she had."

"Beatrice we're in the dark about and Penelope I doubt anybody really got to know."

"Strange, but that's my actual given name."

"That's? That is a strange name. Sorry, I'm into him again. This character called Phew. Excuse me."

"Where are you going?"

"An insert in a story I have to make. Your actual name and the name that's before. I know just where it belongs."

"Don't you ever stop?"

"I don't want to lose it."

"Well, it cut me off."

Walking to the corner with her next morning he sees across the street the woman he used to see nearly every weekday morning last winter and spring walking in the opposite direction from him as he went to work and whom he never spoke to but wrote the story of the remaindered-book-shredding machine operator about.

"Why didn't you introduce yourself then?" Pierian says. "She would have enjoyed hearing you'd been musing and doodling about her so long. And where you finally make a move and meet, mate, marry and what was that, have girl and boy twins the opposite sex of each looking like the other of you?"

"I thought she'd be annoyed. Or petrified. Early morning's the worst time for making introductions. I was always late for school. She seemed in a hurry too. I didn't think women liked learning their lives had been mushed over for six months or tampered with in writing as I'd done, and for possible profit. I'm not sure. Hundreds of excuses. I did once follow her to work, though only for research."

"Say hello now. You must still want to."

"It's over. I got it out."

"Pardon me, Miss. This will have to seem odd to you. Hold on. And don't you also slip away, Paul Clay. You see, my talented friend here who one day is going to be very famous, was accustomed to seeing you religiously every workaday morning for a year and plumed a story about you too that I'm sure you'd be interested in reading before its major publication."

"I'm late," she says. "If you please?"

"No derring-do. Nevertheless, she knows of you now."

"Her voice, backspin and revulsion were how I pictured it. All in all, I'm not disappointed."

He drives his bus to the other side of the street to avoid getting a parking ticket and sees both license plates are gone. He phones the police, is told to come to the precinct, in a room with his back to the detaining cage of sleeping and grumbling prisoners, he sits beside a desk and faces a detective who types the petty larceny report with one finger and asks Paul's profession.

"Two of my namesakes are writers," and he gives their names and titles of some of their books he says he has all of here and home. Paul says he never heard of the men though assumes because of their unusual last name they're brothers.

"Unrelated. I did a check. None to mine either, though before the boat over, who can say? But each a near to superior millionaire from his writing. The younger even younger than you and the screen author and director of his own book for the space movie now at the Embassy here and also a surgeon in his own right—the brains. Inasmuch as they are my namesakes I thought it a goodluck tag for a writer and one that might even have a persuasive factor with the publishers. So February this year I started what you might say to write too. A novel. So far a couple hundred final pages long. Maybe not the tight complex tense work you might like to write—I don't know. Everybody's got to earn a living somehow. But this one about a decent enough kind of tough detective in a hustling vibrant metropolis like our own who goes wrong. He's like me in physiognomy and build through not character, and his office and headquarters are modern and efficient and clean, like ours are to be in the new precinct going up. Like a putz—beautiful home, ideal wife, three kids, untainted record and a father line that goes back six deep with honest city cops, he gets infatuated with one of the prettier young prostitutes he's arresting and winds up pimping and shielding and rejecting his life and family for. But he pays the piper. After a few brushes with the girl's ex-pimp and the mob who don't like anyone weaseling in, cop or not. And conflicts with his captain, police board, commissioner—you know: mayor, buddies, honor, oath, priest, crusading reporters, citizens review and what's in here—inside, besides his retired father and dying momma. I have it where it's the girl's brother who finds out about this same hypocrite cop who once beat the bejusus out of him and booked him for pinching a used two-wheeler a few years before and which started this kid's long road down. He shoots the detective in the confessional booth he's in right after the detective told the priest he was going to quit the force, blow the whistle on himself, serve time in the pen and then resume college and his wife if she will and start a new life. I thought it would make a great television or theater movie. Because most of the TV and movie shows I've seen except *Dragnet*—not the early TV series *Dragnet* but the movie—are what? Big chase, kill, muscle and blood and screw scenes but nowhere from definitive police work and the private fears and frustrations of family life and law enforcement every police officer goes through. They probably never had anyone that close inside to write them."

A policewoman says "Moment, Tom, but how do you fingerprint the right thumb again? Mine keep getting smudged."

Tom takes her thumb, says "Roll it to the left if the thumb you're printing's the right—loosen it up there, loosen—and the other way around for the four other fingers which roll right. Wait, I'll demonstrate," and he signs Paul's slip stating he's reported to the police his license plates were stolen and gets up to fingerprint a prisoner who'd been let out of the cage.

As Paul's leaving the room a man with welts and cuts on his face and dried blood on his clothes screams "Yaaaaaah" as he gropes his fingers through the cage wires.

"Shut up," Tom says.

"He got part of my slip."

"Let's see. What you get so close for? Trying to get the inside dope. All these writers secretly want to be cops."

"It's okay," the policewoman says. "He didn't nip none of the written part. And you, goddamnit. Stay in your stupid cage."

Shelly's not in the stateroom she said she'd be in. A steward reads the passenger list and says if Paul wants to locate an unlisted passenger he must see the purser at ship's stern.

"Paul," Sharon says, running into his arms. "I'm sailing. Mom's letting me go." Stepping off the gangplank next to the purser's office are Shelly and Alain.

"Terrific," Alain says. "Now I can leave you

both with general amnesty." He gives Paul Sharon's Sharon-size Winnie-the-Pooh doll and a bottle of champagne, kisses Sharon and Shelly goodbye and goes.

"Ah, the younger Bustelli," the purser says, bowing and shaking Sharon's hand. "So small. You were this little big when many years ago, now look you've grown. No harness—see? And you, madame, *tout va bien*? Our charts should read another smooth voyage I can safely say."

Sharon and Pooh squeeze into Paul's lap in the lounge outside the purser's while Shelly gets her room changed. A pirate comes on board. A grownup Little Red Riding Hood. A logger, cowboy, hillbilly, hobos, camp counselors, mountain climbers, gypsies, Prohibition gangsters, Merry Pranksters, Neville Chamberlain, a few Blue Angels. Royalty, Trotsky, majordomos, spangled Pueblos, woolly Brahms, wily Shaw, Rasputin, Charles Manson, D'Artagnan, movie starlets, Forties harlots, young F. Scott Fitzeldas, Vampira, lion and tiger tamers, Miss Liberty leading three wee pekingese, van Goghs painting v's for crows, sheep ranchers and their wives, continental spies.

"Oh, I forgot," Sharon says. "I'm told to tell you to come to France soon."

"But I'll be on the *France* to France with you, didn't you know? I'm supposed to swallow you whole. Then the purser'll have to let me on free as you and your ticket'll be inside me."

"Shelly's buying mine now. Did the Multimal ever get away from that hospital?"

"Today. It's too short a tale. That's not the reason he left. I signed the release myself. These hands, Sharon. But the Multimal had no moolah or medical insurance, so they locked him in a subbasement closet till he could pay. He *Je vous prie'd* me. I scrounged around town till I came up with the money, fifty hundred thousand dollars, but when I got back he was gone. Escaped. Kicked the closet door down only to find an iron one, which wouldn't budge, so he picked its intricate lock with his middle horn which can work like a skeleton key. He searched the subbasement floor for an exit. Someone coming, he quickly pretended to be a door, a ceiling pipe, a glucose bottle or oxygen tank, then flat out like a stretcher or linoleum floor strip if he felt this bottle didn't belong in that hall. He ran along corridors, through many doors, up many stairs, past elevators, escalators, nurse's aide stations, till he reached the lobby. With the hospital staff dashing after him. Two big rear ends plopped on his back and a rough hand grabbed his tail and dragged behind him. He was nearly caught. What could he do? He bucked the bodies off his back and tail and galloped through a huge glass door. Now cut, riddled with welts, which are like bumps, blood freckling his face and hide, he got on a lobby mop, for remember, he couldn't fly minus the missing tail he entered the hospital to get and never got, and flapped into the air high above the street. I was down there waving and shouting for him to come back. 'Come back. Now you come right back down here,' I yelled. But it was too late. He'd had it with all of us, he said. 'Now that I've seen you I don't feel bad I didn't say so long, Paul. In fact, I just said "So long, Paul," Paul. But there's nothing new for me on earth so I'm off to try and find what's beyond and write about my life from out there, something you could never do because you never had nor will ever have the proper equipment and distance. I'm sorry, but you'll never see the Multimal again.' Those were his last words. Away he flew. Our Multimal, Sharon dear. A whisk in the sky. A shooting star fizzing out. A blotch, a splotch, a spot, a dot, a midge, a mite, a mote, a pip, dip, nip, nit, then nothing. *Rien*. Gone. *Disparu*. Thin air. *Plein* bare. My eyes searched and said where oh where oh where? Forever."

"The end."

"In a way I'm glad. This has gone on too long. We all need a change. He from me, you from him. Even your mom's getting one—that room. And new characters, new adventures. We need that too. Maybe that's what he'll write about at his journey's end and send back to us through one of his new friends. An interplanetarypal. A galacticgal. Stories of the most innermost secrets and mysteries of the universe and ourselves. If anything, this universal messenger al should be even more fantastic-looking than our beloved hero. A creature created perhaps from the marriage of our crazily-constructed Multimal and whatever he finds by way of female where he's flown."

In French and English the P.A. system voice requests all visitors to leave.

"He's more than a half hour yet," the waiter says, setting beside their champagne ice bucket a platter of crustless baloney tea sandwiches and dish of Spanish nuts.

"If I stuck in a story two thefts on a man's car and his being mugged by men with knives within 14 hours and two pages of one another, the reader would say it's too farfetched to really have happened in a realistic undetective-type story and it couldn't be placed."

"I'll recruit those for my next one and see," Shelly says.

The second announcement so worries Sharon that he won't debark in time that she goes to the promenade desk above the gangplank to watch him leave.

Paul carries the valises and doll to the stateroom and Shelly locks the door. "One more hug before we sail, Paul. It will have to hold me till you come. You will come? Writers must stick together. You can use the *France*. This very room would be nice. All the free wine you can drink. If our schedules work out right I'll be there when you reach port. I think it would be fun if this whole ship were a five-day convention for the members of PEN. Tell the ship's librarian you're my most helpful colleague and he'll reserve for you all the latest novels and magazines in English. My apartment in Paris only overlooks gardens and the French President picnicking with his loyalest subjects and verbs and it has so many rooms you can get lost from or with me for days. If you like I'll find you a French girlfriend. Until I do I'll be your companion if you promise not to groan. It'll be so easy, Paul, easy, and Alain only comes and goes briefly, flying in and out for a *le weekend*. We can go shopping for the rawest goriest horsemeat together in the newest superest soo-puh-mar-kehs. It can be so cheap. You don't have to have lived there to know how. And you need a reprieve after all your hard work. But we better be sharp as the prow's about to pull away. Shh. That last announcement said I am definitely the last. Have we time? I want to keep you aboard. Say you'll come. You'll love it where I am. Good company there is a steal. Say the word and I'll let you work alone for as long as you want. And you know the area well yourself and just think of the pleasure we can have together there. There. Something moved. By God, my Paul, speak low, don't jolt, but something inside me just moved. I think I conceived."

"Nonsense. But I've got to go."

"But one of your heroines said it happened with her husband and then her lover with her first two and that's why she knew she conceived a third time with you."

"I've told you that wasn't me."

"Then your reappearing narrator Page whose experiences mimic yours. 'The zygotic occurrence just occurring' is I think close to what this woman Daisy you said you knew said after you or they made love."

"Rose. 'The zygotic organism just organized.' But she'd never say that. Besides, she was childless when she met me and what she did say is that 'It's very possible because of your erotodesperateness and our genitoprotectoneglectfulness that you've made me in a family way.' I only slipped it into the piece the way I did because I thought it exemplified the queer things people say they're sure they know and feel and occasionally at the oddest times."

"But I did think it happened when Sharon was conceived. I never wrote it up because I never quite believed it. A powerful infinitestimal coming together is how I can best now describe it, which I was told by everyone I told the experience to that it was nonsense. Look seriously at me. Because when it didn't repeat itself till this moment when my tides and moon risings and you have never been so precise, I'm positive it happened both then and now. You will come to Paris."

"Ship's moving."

"Wavering. I haven't heard the chains reraveling or thud of the tug. Christmas, Paul. Fireplace in every womb. Mistletoes on every Mrs.' toes. Alain will be sacking Addis Ababa and the old Congos. Forget the horsemeat: I'll cook you the most sumptuous stuffed goose and mincemeat pie. The American Hospital's the best in Paris. If you like I'll let you be my last husband and sire. Names, Paul, think of names. All characters have names. Now give

Sharon the key and have a steward lead her down."

"Run," Sharon yells. "You can be captured and charged, thrown into the sea. Jump. *Vite.* The boat's taking off. Save him, Pooh Bear," and she throws her doll into the water.

On scrap paper: an antennaeless Empire State Building on its side. A floating cigar, somehow lit in the center, no band or ash. A metal model of an ocean liner telescoped through a bunched-up fist. A wooden imitation of one drifting down the gutter, into the sewer, out of the picture, no trace. A papermade version of one, bombarded into the tub. One of those. None of those. There are of course bands on board, racketing rocky goodbyes and cancan adieus. Nor the man (a cook?) in a white shirt or jacket (kitchen uniform?) singularly and uninterruptedly waving hankies (aprons, dishrags, table linen?) in both hands and with his entire torso outside the tiny porthole to all of us ashore. I wave(d) back. Neither that.

Paul finishes a story he started in Mawkuhpuk. It ends with Pete watching the top forward officer signal to someone that the anchor chains be raised, the dockers unloop the lines from the bollards and the visitors on the street wharf cheer them for their sole effort, a tug nudges the Italian liner out of its berth into the river till it's equidistant with the two New shores, the ship laying for the Atlantic, blowing its brains out, its creeping superstructure still in view above the harbor buildings as he turned for home. He would have used in modified form the stateroom scene with Shelly believing she conceived if he hadn't written a similar scene in the published story Shelly spoke about. Marta had already flown to Rome with her dad.

Downtown, he has three photocopies made of the story and walks to his agent's building nearby.

"Who's there?" a woman says behind the frosted glass door.

"Paul Clay, a client of Robin's. I'm dropping off a new manuscript."

"She isn't in. Shove it under. I'm sorry, sir, but it's only that two of the offices got held up today and I'm still shaking like a leaf. I'll see that she gets this, though."

The original he mails to the editor of a magazine based in Boston that published his first short story seven years ago and gave him a thousand dollars for it and has rejected about fifty since. Attached to the story is a note postdated ten days saying "Dear Paul: This is an engaging story, but the buildup is awfully long for what the piece delivers, and we think it's perhaps too slight, and pat. Thanks all the same for trying us again. Best, Kirt. KP:mn. Enc."

In the Chock Full O'Nuts he always goes to for a celebratory coffee and date nut bread and cream cheese sandwich after he's dropped off and mailed a new story he remembers that *"Quid nunc?"* was also the last line of the story the Boston magazine published.

"Is it possible getting back a manila envelope I pushed through this slot five minutes ago?" he asks the information clerk at the post office.

"I don't know. Let's try. What's the drop-dispatch sheet say? Got a few minutes left. Too bad, it's been picked up before its time. It's your good guess where it's gone now."

He writes another last line, rewrites the last two pages, changes the *Good* in the story's title *Good Copy* to *Bad*, rewrites the first page the title's on, tomorrow he'll send the three revised pages special delivery to Robin and Kirt and ask that the previous first page and last two that came or will come with the story he sent be destroyed.

At his folks' place is a postcard and the past week's mail his mother just remembered she stacked away for him. One's from an editor at a publishing house that's been considering a story collection of his, who begins "Once more, Paul, I have lost, and am heartbroken."

The card from Mawkuhpuk saying "Did I ever say thanks for your invaluable aid and unflagging consideration? Well thanks anew if I did say it wherever I last saw you and have a profitable and prodigal year and you'll write me, alright?"

An animal-cluttered ink-stained letter from Ezra saying "Dear Paulie. I really Papreciate your Book Present and Til likes it too. Please very important you cum visit us and send me all your dimes and quarters and half dollars dated, and everything before that, from 1964. XX, OO, EZ."

An aerogram from his sister in Genoa saying "I've done it again, begun a new uterine chain, can't finish my novel, being bumped from this hovel, lost my inseminating boyfriend and American fellowship, some genoa salami chased me across a dozen parked dinghies to give me a busted lip, got a bodyaching virus, my pretty pickle's the direst, need your pecuniary support, if performable your in-person rapport, so many what-to-do's, don't tell the you-know-who's, though you can mention the IOU's, I send you and ours my god-bless-you's, pity, Kitty."

A letter forwarded from a London quarterly from a lady who "read and with minor qualifications savored your short story and would like to know if you'd be disposed to collaborating on a recipes-I-have-stolen cookbook for stateside consumption. Since your story seemed to be an autobiographic account of a painter turned Surrealist pamphleteer, could I then surmise you're also capable to do the illustrations?"

An invitation from the New York Artists and Writers Williamsburg 9 Defense Committee for a benefit dinner-dance. Among the honored guests will be several Pulitzer and National Book Award winners and two of the nine accused bombers.

A flyer from the Arabian Nights Cleaners suggesting it's time he have all his rugs and carpets cleaned.

A letter from a friend saying "How come no note or call about my novel? I know the publishers sent you a copy months ago and I've seen you on the street myself. I was in a cab and you were running. I had her honk the horn: you didn't stop. I screamed your name: you didn't seem to hear. I wanted to get out: she had to make the light to pick up a new fare. When I finally did get back across the street: you were gone. What's wrong: you didn't like the book? Too embarrassed or busy to give me a few words? Is it you just have something against the novel? I don't mind the truth: but say something at least. Because believe me: if even other writers won't read our fiction and especially when they receive free hardcover copies: who will?"

"You can't imagine what went on here today," his mother says. "First your father. I'll spare you the poison rhubarb. Then the cable TV people galumphing through the apartment into the yard for all the tenants upstairs. Then our unctuous drunk next door yahooing the sunniest obscenities at Dad and I after we had kissed and made up and were enjoying a breather in the shade. And your aunt's eternal telephone miserablies. The young friends of the front tenant ringing our bell every twenty minutes to sniff and snort past the vestibule door. The tympanist who now must be practicing on ten kettledrums in that

saint someone and another church. And my cake. This
heat. The caterpillars. That rottened grubby floor.
I swear if I had your talent I'd write a story about
this neighborhood, family and house. Some day I'm
actually going to sit down and try."